Nick Barlay

Curvy Lovebox

20/20

Published in United Kingdom by *20/20,* 1997
An imprint of The X Press,
6 Hoxton Square, London N1 6NU
Tel: 0171 729 1199
Fax: 0171 729 1771

Printed by Caledonian International Book Manufacturing Ltd,
Glasgow, UK.

Distributed in UK by Turnaround Distribution, Unit 3, Olympia
Trading Estate, Coburg Road, London N22 6TZ
Tel: 0181 829 3000
Fax: 0181 881 5088

ISBN 1-874509-47-6

to SB, for the footsteps

NOTE: "Drug dealers don't enhance the quality of life but they sure as shit helped with writing Curvy Lovebox."

"Drugs don't enhance the quality of life, but they could work with the next 188 pages."

Nick Barlay

Curvy Lovebox

Nick Barlay works as a freelance journalist, writes for Time Out and has had his plays broadcast on national radio. He has travelled the twilight world from Kowloon to Camden and from Tooting to Tangiers and still travels the darker parts of London's underground. Curvy Lovebox is his first novel.

Four am Monday

The music's still pumpin' out the PA as DJ Loopi DexDex makes his last stand. The place empties slowly but my E's rushin'. It's givin' me a hard on that I'm tryina hide by stuffin' my fists in my pocket. She's standin' with this friend who's like a seventies disco chick with more platform than Waterloo. They're both lookin' a bit pasty in the flashin' silver purple light. It's now or never so I go over an' sor'a wedge in between her an' her friend. They ain't dancin' or nothin'. I stick my mouth up close to her ear.

— Don'tcha like the music then?

— Nah it's all tha' jazzy funky shi'. No fuckin' rave music, she says. Band was wicked though.

— Yeah I know'm. They're friends o' mine.

We look at each other. She's alright. Should be in uniform. Small an' glittery with no horns on her head. An' she don't look sick with me either. Over the other side the warehouse Ezra an' Deezee an' Zeb an' the rest o' their grunge metal band *Frontloada* are packin' up. I say to her to wait a second an' go over to Ez. I have to sift through the laggers who just float about til there ain't nothin' left to float about for. Some victim's gettin' stretchered with a crocodile of dancers formin' behind. Another's gettin' mouth to mouth on the stage with steam sweat an' summer heat hangin' above like a poison cloud.

Ez is foldin' up drum stands like he was an action hero with a machine gun. Bein' a short guy his Reebs seem to reach his knees. An' with his bala pulled down to the nose I have to talk to his laughin' teeth.

— Listen man... ask a favour yeah? Got this-

— Yeah I noticed. Want the keys?

— Na mean.

— Iss parked round the uvver side o' Tooley. You got 'bou' four an' a 'alf minutes.

Smilin' I palm the ton of keys Ez is holdin' out.

— Safe.

— Safe? Takes me 'bou' four an' a 'alf to roll one on. I'll time ya.

I go back kickin' through the empty beer cans vodka cocktail an' lucozade bottles all over the floor. She's whisperin' to her friend but they stop when they see me. The swingin' keys do the talkin'. They exchange a smirky look an' she follows pushin' through the sweaty crowd an' out the warehouse.

Down Bermondsey Street there's cabs everywhere fuckin' each other up an' little scuffles breakin' out. A bottle flies but don't seem to land. There's clappin' an' runnin' for no reason. Some guy in nothin' but pants is climbin' a lamppost shoutin':

— WHERE'S MA CROO? WHERE'S MA CROO? WHERE THEY GONE?

Further down two mad fuckers're grabbin' onto each other's t-shirts an' growlin' murder. She takes hold of my hand. I pull her close. We're suddenly together against the chaos goin' down. One driver's openin' up this other cab that's already full.

— YOU WAS MY FUCKIN' FARE. You was all my fare. OUT. Come on. OUT. You're comin' wi' me...Ge' ou' the fuckin' car. Ge' ou' the fuckin' car. Ge' ou' the fuckin' car...

Red an' green lasers splash round catchin' blond ponies skanky beards orange lipstick gold teeth. There's people millin' everywhere. Coolin' off on the pavement. Crashed out on bonnets. Passin' wraps with handshakes. Suckin' down spliff in shadow. Raggamuffins. Ravers. Ruffnecks. HARDCORE GIRLS in black like stormtroopin' death squads. Designer posses worried about tarnishin' up their trainers. A set of Japanese Elvis fans queuin' real patient to get mugged. Even grunge *stoodents* from out of town. An' a loada nobodies to make up the numbers.

We go left toward Tooley Street. The music's fadin' but I can make out *Frontloada's* single: *I tried to reach nirvana but I only got near Kilburn*. I let go her hand an' put my arm round her. Feels like I'm gonna split from the heat. But the air from the river's fresher. Makes me dizzy enough to forget everythin'. I slump over her so's she has to carry my weight. She's laughin' under the strain. Then pretendin' to squeak like a mouse.

— EE EE EE, goes the mouse with each step.

On the corner of Berm an' Crucifix I spot Ezra's red VW van more like dumped than parked an' we cross over.

— Ain't doin' it unless you got a condom, she says.

I unlock the slide an' take this condom out my pocket. It's been down there some time. The wrap's crumpled at the edges. She ain't bothered. She looks at the slide an' I pull it open like it was the entrance to a frilly fuck palace. Instead of a stanky diesel hole.

We clamber in an' try an' get comfy but in the end give up an' go for it right there on a mattress an' a drum stand that won't go out the way. Can't even feel her skin she's wearin' so many t-shirts an' shit. An' in the dark I can't find where her clothes begin. I'm peelin' off stuff that just ain't got no point like a kinda *boob toob* arrangement three layers down with another four to go. But I don't say nothin'.

Neither does she. She's quiet like she ain't even there. One moment or another I can see light in her eyes starin' far off into the dark. I just pull an' grope about somewhere between her washed out pale face an' purple docs.

— You smell of... somethin'...

— Iss jasmine.

— Yeh... nice. Jasmine. But I'll call you Riz ok, I say still tryina make a space in her clothes.

— Wha' for?

— Cos your face glows in the dark like a rizla.

She pulls my head down toward her mouth. I feel the cold of her metal rings on the back of my shaved neck. For a second I can't see the whole thing happenin'. We're mangled in clothes. I just feel the drum stand scrapin' against my shin. Smell of oil an' stale fag ends. Creaks from mattress an' suspension like a daft comedy. Then I'm bonin' away like a crazy dog cos o' the E.

She takes all of this in silence with the drum stand clankin' an' the river flowin' through the yellow dark like forever. Then I'm done. She kinda smiles still pale an' tries to sit up pullin' down her t-shirt. But I stay on top of her rollin' around an' squeezin' her sides til she giggles. Out the blue she says:

— Issem blokes again. Out there...

— Wha'? I'm mumblin'. Wha' blokes?

— Over there by the car.

I get off of her an' squint round through the gap in the slide then out the back window. I'm rollin' off the rubber an' tryin' to pack myself up balancin' on my knees. Two guys with their backs toward us are feelin' around in the boot of their car on the opposite corner. They're in shadow. An' with most of the car out of sight I can't tell who they are.

— Wha' 'bou' 'em?

— They 'ad a loada money on 'em innit. They was wavin' it round the whole time. Ask anyone. They ain't tough or nothin'... D'y'know'm?... Bigger one had a wallet inside... D'y'know 'em then?

I look at her sort of dreamy. I'm well out of it an' still tryina get my dick back in. They're talkin' in low voices that I can't make out. Then one of 'em laughs:

— Gaaaaa.

Koom. Ain't no other laugh like his. An' with him's got to be his brother li'l Joey. Top of Nood's tick list.

— You know'm innit.

She can tell from my face that I do. I look her over wonderin' if all the answers'd just lead to the same thing. Could say I knew 'em real well an' that would be the end of it. Whatever it is.

— Don't really know 'em no. Not really. Friends of friends. Na mean.

— S'you don't know 'em.

I know exactly what she's thinkin'. She looks at me like this is a thing that's got be done. Like it was all a big playground where you can fall over an' the bruises heal up by magic. An' in a way it is. Only there'll be hell to pay. Nood was gonna do 'em for his money after the weddin'. This way... I don't have to say nothin'.

We sit there watchin' 'em for untold time. Riz don't even look at them. Just me. Like I'm supposed to be the one the only one. Only I know she's on a buzz. An' when you're on a buzz there's only you. Koom an' Joey're still fiddlin' in the boot happy go lucky like they was packin' for Cyprus. I try to say som'in that don't commit me but all that comes out is:

— They're bendin' over for it Riz...

— Gonna do it then?

Which is a yes or no sor'a question.

— Issup to me innit...

I'm lookin' them over weighin' it all an' thinkin' no. An' even when I think of them as a coupla dumb cunts for not keepin' an eye out I'm thinkin' no. An' thinkin' 'bout Riz even more no goes through my head. Like a big no cos it ain't for her. It'd be for me. For *my* buzz.

I look up an' down the street. My heart starts goin' an' I tense up when I see it's clear. But even grippin' the handle of the slide like it was the throat of a shitface enemy an' hatin' 'em which is easy I'm still thinkin' no. But Riz knows more about wha'm gonna do than me. She kneels up by the window for the view.

— Don't get out til I tell ya.

— Gonna do i' then? she says like it was still a question.

But I don't move. I can't move. I just know I have to. When I'm ready which is at no point in particular I open the van door quiet as I can. Taste of the river in my mouth. Diesel water. Rank shit. I slip out into the warm air an' just walk up behind 'em. Each step's straight an' silent but gets me no nearer knowin' wha'm gonna do or even if. But somethin's gonna happen. I'm crouchin' more the closer they get. They're too busy. Too fat with themselves to know shit. A second later they're big. There's a spot on Koom's neck. A crease on Joey's shirt.

They don't hear fuck til it's too late. Li'l Joey gets a kick in the nuts from behind an' keels over like he's dead his arms coverin' his head. My teeth're grindin'. Koom tries to turn but he's carryin' too much load round the gut. I just lay into him before he can see my face. Punch him in the head so's he goes down. Then in the nose over an' over with this rage buildin' inside. Three four times. More. His head keeps bouncin' up off of the road every time. Fuck his ass. I mash his fuckin' nose. Fuckin' joker. Mash it good I'm thinkin'. For everythin'. For anythin' anyone ever done to me. He ain't gonna forget by the mornin' after. He ain't gonna forget period. A spotlight off a riverboat spreads shadows cross the street. I can see blood. Only it looks black. Smooth an' thick as tar. Settin' solid on the pavement in the shape of the words *I was here*. It's difficult to know when enough's enough.

They had it comin'. I get another rush off the E. Love an'
peace innit. Sometimes I'm blown out by what I can do.
But they had it comin' an' everyone'll say so. As long as
they don't know it's me. Breathin' like I'm chokin' I look
through for the wallet. Can't hardly grip it cos my
fingers're so tensed. Well fat with paper though. I leaf it
out an' creep back toward Riz feelin' shaken.

But as I reach the van she busts out an' starts runnin' an'
I have to follow her down the street like a fool. Middle of
the fuckin' night an' we're runnin'. Can't believe it. We
don't look back til we're almost at the warehouse an'
mingled in again. There's cops arrived further up tryina
sort the night from the comin' day. Nobody pays no
attention to us. Riz don't even ask if I'm ok or what. Just
stops out of breath an' starts gigglin' like issall a big laugh.
I pull her into a doorway keepin' my back to the people.

— Iss loads innit, Riz goes.

— Yeah a wedge.

— Told y'I saw it. Gi's some then.

I peel off a coupla twenties an' give 'em over but she
don't look happy.

— Za' all you're givin' me?

So I give her another an' balls the rest. She's lookin' at
her money about to open her mouth again.

— Thass i' Riz baby... Sixty's go'a be enough for your
piggybank. I done the work.

— 'Salright, she shrugs, ain't savin' i'. Skank off school
an' go up the West End or som'ing.

— Yeah? Like a bi'a muggin' an' shoppin' before your
porridge do you?

— Wha'? You're well weird.

Then she starts to go all mushy. I can see it in her face.
Like a droopin'. Dreamy eyes lookin' up at me.

— D'y'want my phone number then?

— No. Bu' gi's i' anyway, I joke.

She says she's got to whisper it in my ear so I let her. Only the bitch blows a mega raspberry in it an' splits fast as she can for her crew. I clean out my ear an' yell:

— DON'T GO BLABBIN' Y'FUCKIN' HEAD OFF.

But I know she's gonna. Just hope it ain't north of the river. They never seen my face. Better not have. They'll turn up at Nood's weddin' an' if it clicks with them... But it won't. They'll just count their teeth offa Tooley Street an' nobody'll know cos they'll have some flash story set for their reputation. I take the keys back to Ezra rememberin' the van's still open.

The band's just startin' to lug the gear out. Deezee with keyboards. Zeb with a guitar on his shoulder. Roadies with silver boxes. An' Jace an' Daisy catwalkin' an' laughin' in harmony. The crowd's all bugeyed. Everyone's checkin' 'em out an' steppin' aside like they was headpriests with lightnin' comin' out their asses. Fola's with 'em a juiced up cab driver from Peckham trackin' the comin' an' goin' with a bottle of montezuma gold in his hand.

— Call tha' four an' a 'alf? says Ez grinnin'.

I flip the keys into his palm.

— She got the extras innit.

— Yeah? Gi's the brochure sometime. I could do with a few ideas.

Fola leans in close laughin' in spurts with tequila drippin' from his fuzzy chin an' love beads swingin' from his neck.

— A'right man you ah really working in tha coalmine. You know what I mean. Like you see jost one thing and you jost go foh it and nothing else can mattah. Really smashing. Really groovy. Babes everywhere man firing vibes. Jost pahtee atmosphere. Body language. Play tha game. Coalmine feeling. To-tahly smashing. One way ticket to pa-ra-dise. Discostyle. Smashing and totahly groovy. Anyone foh a cab?

Ez an' me look at each other.

— You mobile or you wanna ride up Kilburn? he says pointin' to the crowd troopin' down to the VW.

Before I can answer Zeb's there takin' off his soaked red sweatshirt his face screwed angry an' his funky twists lookin' soppy as seaweed.

— That was the worst fuckin' gig we ever done an' you know wha'-

— Fuck off we's blindin' innit, says Ez lookin' at me.

— They was bangin' with you man, I say reassurin' him.

— See wha'm sayin'? If he's sayin' they was bangin' they was bangin' an' we's blindin' so don't gimme no *negativity* shit specially righ' now when we're rockin' an' the crowd is gaggin' for your cheesy smile. Innit.

But Zeb looks more likely to buy sensible tupperware than this shit.

— The light man missed *all his fuckin' cues*. I's riffin' in a fuckin' cellar rudeboy.

— Well nobody threw nothin' at the stage so wha' the fuck you want a poncey slowhander to round it off?

Zeb just spit on the floor an' skulk off seekin' other consolation.

— He'll get over it, Ez grins. So you comin' or wha'?

— Nah safe. I had 'nough o' drum stands for one night y'na mean.

— Yeah an' you got Nood comin' on strong innit. Get this: I asked 'em why they's leavin' early an' Nood goes: *I need my beauty sleep.*

We crease up with Ez repeatin' the line a few times for the extra mileage. I could do with a ride bad cos it's a long walk for me an' I ain't got my car but I can't face the shit I go'a talk with the band. The moanin' 'bou' each other an' the heavy duty politics like they was warlords carvin' empires of sound. Me an' Ez shake an' I'm about ready to go.

But Fola slaps my back grinnin'. He lifts his tequila toward my mouth which I open wide with joy. He pours a good long shot down my throat. It hits the spot so good I have to grab the bottle out his shakin' hand an' take another an' another til Fola sobers swipin' it back.

— Hey shitface tequilagroovah-

But by then I'm flyin'. I give the resta the band a wave like I ain't got a care.

— La'ers.

— Yeah, says Ez, Nood's magic moment...

Five or so

I sift an' star' walkin' headed for Tower Bridge. There's small groups of people amblin' down tryina keep their party vibe goin' long as they can. Swearin' they had the best time. Pickin' up flyers an' exchangin' grapevine facts like the where an' the when of the next one. But one by one group by group they're peterin' off into sidestreets or stoppin' off for night buses or rememberin' where they parked. Until I'm alone.

The dawn's comin' up pale orange over the river. For a while the thumpin' pavement makes my ears ring with music an' fear an' raspberries an' the fucked up noise of livin'. Then crossin' the bridge I'm tiny an' nothin' like fly shit with the city fanned out in front an' the towers above still dark from night. I walk but can't hear my feet like I ain't got weight or I ain't even there.

On the bank below the bridge a police boat's swayin' on the current with gulls hangin' above. Two cops with a long hook're strugglin' to haul some shape onto the deck. The shape's heavy sodden an' they go'a work. But there's no noise. Like they're lifeless only swayed by the current with the gulls just hangin' an' the dawn comin' up. Across the other side of the bridge only cats an' bin lids break the silence. Somewhere.

I avoid Aldgate. Always some shit goin' down. A junction where cleanin' crews underground staff an' lawmen hang out tryina make up as many questions as they can for the public they're gonna meet the next day. Go down Petticoat Lane instead. A twisted metal frame's been left abandoned by a stallholder from yesterday's market. There's market trash on the street an' in my head. The edge of the city. Cheap an' nasty. Pass Liverpool Street an' out onto Moorgate wonderin' what to do.

On Moorgate the street sweepers're out doin' their own tiny patches. Like bit by bit they're gonna sweep the world. I shuffle along wired an' hungry at the same time. There's a lush in a trenchcoat that I smell from down the street. He's doubled into a bin rootin' for treasure. Only he ain't movin' so I stop to see if he's dead. But lookin' close as I can he still don't move. So I give his coat a pull. His widemouth smokey face pops out like a gallery duck.

— The nurse hit me.

Then he grins. All along traffic lights're changin' back an' forth for no reason. I reach Finsbury Square an' crash on a bench brained. There's bright light comin' up. Too bright. I half close my eyes. Somethin' moves by a tree. I pass out. A drill wakes me. They're diggin' the square with their asses hangin' out. A deckload of faces is watchin' from the two seventy one. Briefcases are herdin' past. Traffic's crawlin' with heat risin' off of bonnets. The air's thick with sun.

I slip down Moorgate tube in a daze an' just go with the emergency flow. Jam in the turnstyle behind some skirt an' blouse accountant. She pro'ly feels my dick an' jumps but by then we're through an' headed for the bottleneck at the escalator.

Stand on the right it says but with people stood on the left as well I'm pushin' through. I use my elbows an' shoulders suddenly rushin' down for the platform like the last train home was ready pullin' out. I can't help it. Only there's a million other elbowin' fucks that beat me to it. They get down on the platform first suits mussed an' puffed with victory.

But the only trouble is there ain't no train. Ain't even due. Ain't even known to be due. An' nobody bats an eye when they see they been stampedin' for nothin'. Elbowin' for nothin'. Bustin' their dodgy fuckin' tickers for nothin'. Cos now we go'a face the fact of it together: there ain't nothin' on the tracks 'cept the reflections of secret mice.

Ten to eight

On the northern line between Euston and Camden in a cloud of black dust trapped in the carriage I get to feelin' kinda edgy like one of them wild killers about to do his thing. Just waitin' for the opportunity. The carriage is full. Like every hour's a rush hour. Only nobody's rushin' cos the fuckin' train's stopped dead an' has been for near 'nough ten minutes.

This is grievous luck since I have to get the car by eight fifteen latest. An' Nood don't fuck around with quarter hours. To him eight fifteen ain't sixteen an' so on. With him gettin' hitched at five an' me bein' the best man there's more'n enough to do. Like business. Nood'll be charged up an' spreadin' pressure everywhere like a cat pisses. An' the thing with Koom an' Joey's just another thing on top.

Some slaphead baby next to me's chokin' on a lolly. The mother don't even wipe the drool off. Slickers slobs rappers an' even a green punk from planet rebel draw away. Nobody wants drool on 'em. But in the heat an' stench of crotch an' periods an' perfume it don't make no difference. Everyone's shiftin' an' fidgetin' tryina make an inch extra air space.

Behind me a coupla loony toon types pro'ly homeless shitheads from Mersey start arguin' in whispers an' really get on my tits. Every fat ear's tunin' in while eyes're pretendin' to read about blood an' death in black and white.

— Ya cuntprick, one's sayin' with harsh breath, ya sang to the fuckin' rozzers. Didn't ya? Sang like a fuckin' canary ya cuntprick. Didn't ya?

— I nev-

— Ya did ya cuntprick canary. You sang and sang like a fuckin' canary ya cuntprick. All the way to the rozzers an' ba'. Didn't ya?

— I nev-

— Ya did you're a cuntprick canary...

Whispers an' rustlin' papers. It's like a carriage-full of hearts starts beatin' faster. We's all clearin' our lumpy throats. I'm tryina think how some tv cop'd deal with them. Pro'ly squint at them an' on the count of three they'd shit their pants. The situation'd change. Things'd move on somehow. The train would move. The next bit would come. I tap on the handrail to make things go faster. Nothin' happens.

— Sang like a fuckin' canary an' you'll be singin' again' ya-

Then I knuckle the handrail an' still nothin' 'cept that they turn up the volume.

— I'm tellin' ya I nev-

— CUNTPRICK... CANARY... GOBSHITE... You're a cuntprick canary gobshite is what you are no two ways.

— I swear I-

— Ya singin' tweetin' rozzer lickin' canary we all know how canaries DIE.

I'm gettin' wound up like I'd warned them but they just won't shut their freakin' mouths.

— ...sang an' sang an' sang didn't ya... Didn't ya. DIDN'T YA.

Then I wait an' wait with the train an' everyone still standin' an' still they're blabbin'. Right behind me. Can feel the waves of air from their guts on my neck. Dogbreath. I feel like I go'a deal with these fuckers. Like issall waitin' for me. Like all eyes're on me. Like they can see I'm tensed up for it. Like they can all see that. So I slip a sharp little screwdriver out my pocket an' hold it down there. Thigh level. Then I edge round in the crowd to face the two of them. The bigger gobshite is pokin' the singin' canary. Right in his face. Pokin' on every other word.

— *Sang* to the *rozzers* didn't ya? Ya *cun-*

Two teenage shiteheads both of them banged up like they was *big an' tough an' livin' rough*. Squirmin' now.

— ...'kin' 'ell... Fucksat for ya bastard?

The tool must've appeared like from nowhere right under his nostril. That's how Jake Gittes gets it in Chinatown.

— Fuck d'y'think iss for? Cunt.

Total silence all round. He's well shitted. An' canary's flapped into the background to leave him to it. He's shrinkin' by the second. Pinhead eyes on the tip of the tool. Clammy clenched fists held in fear to his tits. Then I see what's really scared him. There's dried blood on my knuckles.

— Wha'... wha' d'ya... want wi' me then?

— Fuck d'y'think I want? Cunt.

His mug makes a massive twitch with all the crap drugs he's ever done an' all the Thunderbird he's ever thrown up in doorways.

— I'll shurri'. Orright? Ok?... Ok?... 'Kin' 'ell... Fuckin' 'ell. I'll shurri' me. I'm no... I don't... I don't just... shite... talk... I don't... that's just me. Orright? I'm gone. Ok?

The tool disappears back down below. I turn my back an' stare out at the black pipes in the tunnel. Laid over them is my curvy image on the glass of the train door. I notice my flies're undone. How long that's been the case I don't know. I do them up an' arrange myself. Touch my face an' hair catchin' a hundred smells on my fingers like Riz an' smoke an' sweat an' oil. Rub the bristle on my neck. Fan my t-shirt to get some air underneath. Let my heart go calm again.

Fuckin' assholes all of them. Soft spongy easy meat. I'm sick of 'em. Their weakness. They wake up thinkin' they're tough enough only to find a whole loada other people's woken up with the same idea. All assholes just waitin' to see who's the biggest motherfucker there is. From Harlesden Stonebridge Kilburn Tottenham or wherever across the north west zone. They'd fight you for nothin'. An' if you got a *business ting* goin' even half a thing they're on you. An' you just go'a be up for protectin' it. Most're phoney cuntpricks. Apart from Nood. But it's not always easy to tell. You just take things as far as you can is all. 'Ventually everyone fits in one level or other.

Then the train's budgin' along with electric blue lightin' the tunnel wall. It gets into Camden an' we all filter out much slower an' quieter than ever hopin' if there's a god he ain't never gonna put us in the same carriage again. I sift fast through the crowd takin' in the open bags an' pockets wishin' my fingers were fast too. Siftin's really wha'm good at. Movin'. Skankin'. Disappearin'. Doin' anythin' an' stayin' free.

The escalator takes me up into the sun. Shopwindows cars flash in my face. Outside people're squattin' up on the rail. Some with their two dollah wares an' shit stapled to big pieces of cardboard. A bracelets in a briefcase guy with nervy eyes. A padded up rollerskater in a helmet. Behind me I hear a collector shoutin' for my ticket:

— YOU WITH THE T-SHIRT, he calls like that really singles me right out.

Bu' I ain't turnin' round. Ain't even reactin'. Fuck should I. Just walk on innit. Thing is I got this motto that a friend once said:

— *Me come from Kilburn. Me don't pay.*

Not that he came from there. Fact he came from most places an' travelled to the rest where Kilburn didn't mean nothin' to nobody. But it was the way he said it. Like it made perfect sense. For me it was only later that it did.

Eight fourteen

There's a breeze blowin' papers an' shit all over. People're sat on the pavement with all this litter clingin' to 'em. Rubbin' dirt in their eyes an' swallowin' it like it was their birthright. I cross the main strip that flushes through Camden like a scabby vein. Weekends it carries in a million losers. Washes 'em up on the pavement so's they can spend their slave wage. Then drains 'em out leavin' broken beer glasses kentucky cartons an' no refunds. Weekdays every bar's got its *happenin' crowd*. You can wear a fake tan down the Brasserie. You can spill someone's pint at the Frog and Gusset. You can be a scumbag down the Ponce Bar. Take your choice. They already taken your peas.

I go through the Inverness Street market. Centrefuckin'stage among the fruit an' veg is some jerk in leather trousers takin' pictures of a model with a tape bangin' out some tinny beat for her to pose to. Behind her people's just starin'. Some want to be like her. Part of the scene. Envyin' the clothes off her back. Envyin' the attention she's got from the ass-lickin' clipboard crew. Others just wanna touch her crack where her leopard spots disappear. But whoever they are all these watchin' faces they're gettin' left in the frame. For the reality factor I guess.

Do a right onto Arlington an' have to step over a loada rot from the market just to get to Nood's gate. I swing it open. Piled in a pigeon shit corner there's some loser from the halfway house that backs onto Nood's. If Camden's got a soul it's in room seven smellin' of piss. Anyway I step over the fuck as he shouts at me from the floor.

— Issall ones an' firkin' zeros ya li'l shitebag.

A Super T rolls out his floppy hand. From above I hear Nood screamin' as I'm climbin' the fire escape.

— MAAC! Shut up! Shuuuut up! You fuckin' parrot! You fuckin' parrot!

Nood spends most of his life choppin' up weed or screamin' at Mac. The bird stands 'bou' three foot an' squawks *na mean* after pretty much everythin' Nood says. Which is often na mean as it goes. I knock an' hear him comin' with his hundred keys an' all these locks an' latches and catches an' shit turnin' an' him still screamin'.

— MAAC! Shuuut up! Shut the fuuck up! Maaaac! 'Ow's it goin'? I tell you wha' man: don't ever get a parrot. Na mean.

— Trust me Nood, I say fixin' a grin. So... the big day...

— Don't fuckin' start man. I fixed y'mo'or up. I'll just get-

— Tea an' a spliff?

— No way. No time. Wipe y'feet an' just go through, he says turnin'.

We start toward the livin' room if you can call it livin'. Issall tools old teabags an' springs up the ass in there. Permanent night on account of blankets nailed across the windows so's Mac don't go gettin' ideas about the big outdoors. Smells of food an' feet an' weed. But ten grand's worth of stereo's rigged up on special racks an' diy units. Speakers like coffins. Woofers an' tweeters growin' all over like mushrooms. Two walls of vinyl an' cd. All for Nood's sounds. But for the first time ever there ain't nothin' playin'. Only sound is Nood throwin' cushions off the sofa real frantic lookin' for somethin'.

— It's tight man. You go'a drive me down the city an' back. I got the rest of 'em Es to shift an' a loada the pukka polynesian na mean.

Polynesian's what Nood says he has when he don't know what the fuck he does have. His idea of a pitch. Thing is I have to stand there lookin' heavy while he pitches to someone mega heavy. Maybe Nood takes me along on these things cos I'm gettin' to look like him. Sleazy an' *stoopid*. How'd that happen? I mean sometimes I catch myself in a shop window or som'in' an' in a certain light from a certain angle I got this look. I'm kinda tall but catch myself lookin' hunchback. Bein' mashed don't help. Round my eyes there's scratches an' lines and rings. An' in 'em there's fuck knows. Everythin's goin' saggy round my thick nose.

— Can't fuckin' find it..., Nood's mutterin'. Si' over there Tax.

Nood points over to a stool an' I try to look comfortable on it. Maybe I do look sleazy but compared with Nood... Fuck. They all say he looks *bad*. He's always paranoid he don't look heavy enough. But his mug's a war zone. Burnt out on whizz. Greased up on chinese takeaways. He's HIV in scabby jeans. An' the gaff stinks o' parrot cak with a lot o' the furniture devastated durin' Mac's outin's from his cage. The big time. Really. Then the toilet flushes. Nood's missus-to-be big Stell comes out all mussed up blond in a bright green dressin' gown like she just got up. She folds her arms.

— Nood you been pukin' again?

— Wha' you on abou' now? says Nood pullin' his empty hand out from down the sofa.

He avoids lookin' at Stell grabbin' his trainers instead. They're still laced an' he's squeezin' 'em on. Stell just stands her ground.

— Stinks to fuck in there. You musta puked. He pukes all the time after a rave. Did 'e tell ya abou' i'?

— I was there Stell.

— Oh yeah course you was Taxi. We left early. I was well ou' of order innit.

Stell laughs. She calls me Taxi on account of me drivin' Nood round the whole time. But it stuck an' these days everyone says it. People take the piss an' snap their fingers when they're ready to go. I can take a joke an' that but when it comes down to it it's a get tough or die sor'a name. Nood jumps up stampin' his trainers into place an' lookin' sour grapes at Stell.

— Babes: I never puked. I ain't puked the las' three raves I told ya.

— You're jokin'. That's your way o' tellin' if they was any good innit.

— Las' three I ain't puked. Righ'?... RIGH'?

— You did.

— I fuckin' never. Not the last three an' I'll tell you why.

With her cheeks sucked righ' in Stell's examinin' her nails this way an' that.

— Yeah go on 'en.

— I controlled the burps that's why.

Stell looks at me an' I scratch my nose. I can hear Mac beakin' round his cage.

— Thass wha' i' was before. The burps.

— Listen to 'im. Oh yeah Nood i' was the burps. Wha' abou-

— Fuckin' listen bitch. Before righ' I was swallowin' air an' it got trapped here.

Nood lifts up his t-shirt pinches some gut an' looks at us both.

— Ah did i' get trapped down there did i'.

— Fuckin' listen-

— Course the pukin's fuck all to do with the two gees o' whizz he does for breakfast. An' an E on top.

— It was the burps.

— Still stinks in there though innit.

— Fuckin' bitch.

Nood bags up two kees of the weed stomps about grabbin' his keys an' arrangin' his bollocks an' kickin' anythin' in the way includin' Mac's cage.

— An' i' wasn't two gees no fuckin' way. I done point two then point two then another point two thass point six yesterday... Can't fuckin' find—

— *Two gees two gees two gees* , Mac squawks.

— See told ya, goes Stell foldin' her arms.

I have to hide my face.

— Don't you fuckin' laugh. Don't you fuckin' star' na mean. Fuckin' birds, says Nood. Ah fuck i'...

Nood disappears through a busted cupboard which is the entrance to a million stash holes. Stell pulls a spliff from a jar on a shelf an' eases herself into an armchair with a leg drapin' over the side.

— Was savin' this for la'er...

She waves her thumb at the cupboard.

— ...Like after Doc Braindead's gone.

I smile as she sparks up an' draws deep five time like she was on oxygen. She passes it over to me holdin' in the smoke then blowin' out slow as she talks.

— One spliff an' the day's gone innit. *How come you missed your own weddin' Stell?* Oh sorry I got stoned in front of the tele innit. Great way to start married life yeah: wrecked with chop suey infestatin' the bowl.

— Could be worse, I go passin' back the spliff.

Stell leans forward to take it throwin' a wave of hair out her face an' drawin' another five time.

— Thass exac'ly wha' I'm worried abou' innit. Sor' him out for us will you Tax cos I can't have him on his usual bender. One day in his life y'na mean. One time he's go'a level out. Calm him down. Talk some sense an' all tha'...

I'm smilin' noddin' sure why not. Stell picks at somethin' on her bare leg checkin' for stubble. There's rummagin' comin' from beyond the hole in the cupboard.

— Nood: wha' y'lookin' for in there?

— 'Salrigh' found i', says Nood emergin' with plaster dust in his hair.

He holds up a tape grinnin'.

— Me sounds innit.

— Bless his cotton socks eh, goes Stell, even if they do belong under concrete.

I'm grinnin' when Nood grabs me under the armpit an' starts haulin' me to my feet splutterin' out the words.

— Come on man load up load up. Go'a cane i' now. Runnin' well late. Well fuckin' late babes. Cos o' *you*.

— Me? Shouldna wasted time lookin' for that then.

We start movin' to the door which sets Mac off.

— *Na mean na mean na mean.*

— Oh sweet. You're off. An' who's gonna sor' out the bog?

— *Na mean na mean na mean.*

— La'er babes, says Nood openin' the door.

— Don't forget you're doin' the right thing at five. Town hall. An' make sure everyone knows for la'er cos-

— Yeah babes yeah alrigh'.

— You be'er ge' 'im there Taxi.

— Don't worry. La'er Stell.

Eight twenty five

Reachin' back inside for a second Nood grabs his scuzzy black an' red bomber jacket with *RR* stitched on the back. Then he locks everythin' he can lock behind him an' clips his keys to his jeans. We go down the yard which is one big oil slick. Nood's still got his *Repairman of the Week* sign nailed up from when he used to work at Jiffy Lube an' Tune.

Below it there're car parts everywhere. Exhausts doors hubs wings wheels. An engine chained up on a makeshift ramp. Middle o' this shit's my car lookin' like an army of psycho panel-beaters been at it all night. I pick my way through avoidin' the grease. Start up the car hopin' it ain't gonna combust in my face. Nood opens the gate an' I back out slow. The lush is still there dozin'. Nood grabs him by the legs an' drags the bundle out onto the pavement without wakin' him. Then he checks out the street both ways an' locks up with a heavy duty chain.

Soon's Nood gets in the car he sticks on his tape. Always the same fuckin' thing. Thassa thing I could never figure 'bou' Nood. Deedees're always paranoid about everythin'. About the cops or other dealers or customers or friends o' friends. About the phone ringin' or not ringin'. About people in coats. About people without coats. An' even about Johnnie Gimp in orthopaedic shoes on the high street. Then Nood gets in a car an' iss windows down an' techno blarin' out at three hundred bpm:

DOG DOG TSSS DOGGA DOGGA DOG TSSS.

Whole fuckin' high street lookin' daggers. He just turns to me an' grins.

— Rave man.

Down back of Camden behind some rancid bus. Then York Way behind some rancid truck. Disused petrol station. Rail lines. Gas tanks. The sun burns my fingers through the windscreen. I get a little rizla of sulph off Nood to swallow down an' keep me goin'. Least it bolts my eyes to the road. Left onto Copenhagen. Through to Penton then right an' on to Angel. City Road to Old Street. Nood's on the mobile the whole time organisin' ahead like there's no tomorrow. Maybe for him there ain't. He's more uptight than usual.

— ...So wha'm I the friendly fuckin' buildin' society? Want a letter 'bou' it: *Dear Sir...* up yours sincerely. Cunt... No... No... I said I'd front it bu' iss go'a be the premier na mean. None o' the formula- Wha? You're breakin' u- wha'?... I-... Wha?... I said none o' the formula... Wha' d'ya mean why? Cos I get a better hit off of your sister's pussy dandruff thass why... Wha?... Oh yeah well fuck you, says Nood cuttin' off the caller.

He punches out another number an' cranks up the tape.

— Alrigh' Kings... Yeah I'm hangin' in there... Yeah I know iss ma big fuckin' day, Nood says screwin' his face at me, ...Abou' tha'... Yeah no sweat Kings I know I do an' I'm workin' righ' now... Yeah man seen na mean... yeah I told you already: if he can earn ou' of i' issup to him innit.... Yeah yeah la'er Kings.... Yeah I'll bell ya.... Yeah I'll bell ya la'er.... I'll-.... Cos I'm on fuckin' location thass why.

Nood slams the phone down against the handbrake.

— Shit my mobile, he says strokin' it.

— Kingsley want?

— Fuckin' 'ell. Supposed to be chillin' today na mean an' everyone like Kingsley's givin' me a headache. Callin' in my liquid which I ain't got cos iss liquid na mean. Ain't even had breakfast yet. Tell ya somethin': Kings was askin' 'bou' the rave when he phoned this mornin' so I told him he missed the best yet innit an' he goes: *that's what you said last time.* I go: so wha'. Y'na mean. I tell ya man the guy don't know livin' from bein' alive...

I nod knowin' Nood wouldn't be mouthin' like that in Kingsley's face. He'd be askin' Kingsley for extra time. Beggin' him. Firin' out mindbendin' excuses about how he was all set to wipe the slate only the people that owe him have all got tragedies goin' down in their lives. *You'll never believe this Kings...* Yeah in front of me he can big himself up all he likes. Make flash arrangements an' dream on.

But it's only a matter of time before he hears about the dickhead brothers. Nood'll pro'ly claim it was him. Like a lot of people Koom an' Joey're only liked to their face. Everbody'll be tryin' to figure whodunnit. There's plenty of guys coulda done it an' probably woulda. Lendon an' that lot. Ezra. Moranni. Vijay an' them. Ame. Keef. An' so on. Plenty. An' the way they was tryina pull a coupla ropey grunge chicks everyone woulda been thinkin' the same thing: cunts. An' when you're loaded you start gettin' ideas. Last night there was a lot of ideas about. Chances are I just got to them first.

Crawl up to the Old Street roundabout. Roadworks an' diversions an' shit lead out every which way. Everyone's jammin' in an' nobody give a fuck. Company time. I look at Nood. He's collectin' spit in his mouth an' leanin' out the window. He's fucked for his money now. Koom an' Joey didn't have it for him no more. An' I couldn't just give it him. Not now. There'd be hell. Pro'ly either way.

Nood gobs. I realise he's just gobbed over another car. Some suit in a fleet car. The guy keeps his head down an'

pretends to fiddle with the radio. Nood's out the car
bangin' deathbeats on the fuck's window.

— You fuckin' cunt I'll muller ya. Y'LISSNIN'? Y'fuckin'
lissnin'?

— Nood. Fuck's sake... Get in.

I glance in the rear view. Nood starts to reach inside his
jacket. It's a real bag of tricks in there. But this time Nood's
makin' moves just for effect an' he gets back in an' the
traffic rolls on. Three feet.

— NOOOD. Fuck's sake man... *Whassamaddawichoo?*

— *Whassamaddawimee? Whassamaddawichoo?*

We start laughin' with the sulph workin' overtime on my
guts an' my teeth an' stretchin' my laugh 'cross both ears.
We're laughin' like this all the way into the backstreets off
of Old Street where the traffic don't really go. I turn into
Rivington an' pull up behind a metal sheet that still closes
off an old buildin' site. First stop's the fat fucks. Never
quick. I pull out the gear from under the back seat.

Nine seventeen

— Answer the fucker.

Nood presses on the bell hundred time. 'Ventually a window opens on the fourth and Bullshitsky's three hundred pound Polish head looks out all puffy from potato salad an' red-eyed from smokin' down buds of skunk.

— Easy wid dat donger man.

— Well what's the hold-

— Hey: you ring one time is all it takes mudder. We're musicians.

— Ring one time fuck, Nood shouts. Three rock stars from transylvania an' you're all stone deaf y'cunts.

— Hey: fokk you know. We was all hasbeens.

— Chuck us down the keys man.

He throws the keys leanin' further out an' lowerin' his voice.

— Hey: middle of a game man. Y'know'm sayin'.

Another fuckin' game. Bullshitsky an' his dinosaur homeboys Shuddupsky an' Gettouttamafacesky they just sit in the kitchen playin' chess all day. An' decidin' the universe. An' bustin' everyone's balls. So by the time me an' Nood go up they're already talkin' theory.

— I checkmated you man, says Shuddupsky pickin' on his ear.

— De fokk you tokkin' about? I was blockin' you out wid ma fokkin' horsey, says Bullshitsky takin' his seat.

Nood sits with 'em an' I just hang back arms folded.

— You're tot'ly fokked in de head, says Getouttamafacesky, his bitch was guardin' all de fokkin' squares left an' fokkin' right.

— Hey: de fokk you tokkin about? I'm gettin' de door an' he's takin' de moves. Ain't it Nood?

— Didn't see nothin' man.

— You was sittin right der sucker. Whatchoo tryin' to say: you was wid your mudder all night?

Bullshitsky starts laughing an' it sets the others off.

— Shit. I am listenin' out for dat dong man, says Shuddupsky, cos you always sayin' how you cannot hear de fokker. An' while I am listenin' you playin' d' fokkin' game.

— Listen to dis li'l fokker. Hey Nood, you hear dat? says Shitsky attachin' a roach clip to his spliff.

— Yeah yeah. Look: you was after the boom poly an' I got two kees.

— Orrright man. OK. Easy... But there ain't nuthin' *boom* about dis poly. Smokes like hair from your mudder's ass. What happen to the hydro Thai or even de Thai *stick* or de lunatic Durban or dat sticky fokkin orange skunk you keep promising and dat most of fokkin town is smokin' an' dat you ain't never delivered?

— Lissen cunt: you want some fuckin' gear or you wanna go on the fuckin' wagon the rest of your days cos I don't–

— I'll take it. I'll take it. I said so. Just makin' a li'l conversation...

They all laugh til they're winded then pull up their joggin' pants at the same time leanin' well back til their laughin' comes to a stop. It's like they have to rest after every joke. Take five. Have a cuppa. Nood lets the whole thing go. He's just waitin' for a better moment. Shitsky stubs out his roach opens a little sidewindow dredgin' up green from his lungs.

— Orright man, he says gobbin' out the window, let's *do* some work.

The table in front of him's laid out with a real sense of order like a dentist's. There's scissors for cuttin' up cardboard roaches. A counterpunch for pokin' in the end of the spliffs. Transparent bags in neat piles accordin' to size. Backup matches just in case some fucker skanks his three clipper lighters in different colours. Scales weights a finger balance a razor a long out of date credit card a magnifying glass an' a special headband with a light on it for close up work. Whatever that is.

— Should be takin' it easy today, says Shitsky workin' the scales. Ain't right gettin' all fokked op on the day you's hitchin' op. Skin op a li'l bud an' get blasted. Know'm sayin'? A li'l kuf spliff an' jos' *chaaarge*. Am I right?

Shuddupsky passes a spliff to Nood who just passes it to me without smokin'.

— Yeah righ'. But the people need sor'in.

— I *hear* you. What time we all got to be at d'church?

— How many times I go'a tell ya? Ain't the church man. Town 'all Euston Road at five. Don't forget you're playin' the toons. Where's your sax?

— Don't worry I got it, says Shitsky fingerin' on his chest an hummin' like he's playin'. *Doo doo do do. Doo da do do...*

— Yeah alrigh'. Sor' us ou'. I go'a chip, says Nood wound up.

— Hey: get Nood his due.

— You got d'fokkin' money in your pants, says Shuddupsky.

— Heh... you say so.

— I know so. You're too fokkin bozzed to know shit.

— *I'm* too bozzed?

We have to listen to this. An' wait. Then listen some more an' wait some more. You interfere with their thing you'd be in deep before you knew it arguin' about whose move it was. Besides with their eight hundred a week orders they's all good friends of Nood. But I seen friendships come to grief on account of tick. An' these guys'd more tick than brains. I see Nood's thinkin' along the same lines. There's some money appearin' on the table. But it's all fives an' tens which don't look good.

— Better count it, says Shitsky, cos I stiffed you again.

He creases up in marijuana giggles tryina keep a big toke down an' endin' up coughin' his guts out. The others follow suit so pretty soon they're all slappin' each other's backs. Nood gathers up the notes an' counts them grindin' his teeth to dust.

— Hey Nood man: kiddin' orright?

— After today I'm collectin'. Na mean?

— Sure thing Nood, says Shuddupsky lookin' round for back-up. Sure thing. Ain't it?

— Yeah absofokkinlutely, says Getouttamafacesky.

— Sure as I'm bozzed, nods Shitsky.

Nood snaps out every note while they all pitch in tryina mess up his countin' by gruntin' out random numbers or askin' each other the time in minutes an' seconds. I just been standin' there through the whole thing sayin' an' doin' nish. But as I turn to go to the toilet my arms drop an' Shitsky catches sight of my hand. After a second he follows.

— Hey: accident or somtin' man?

— Yeah righ'.

We go along this narrow corridor with Shitsky's shoulders knockin' pictures on both sides. By the time we get to the loo a few steps later he's pooped.

— You go raving last night? he says breathless.

— Shoulda come man, I say takin' a leak.

— Too old an' fat for dat shit. Know'm sayin'?

— Get into shape. Y'start steamin' like a pressure cooker just gettin' off your ass innit.

— Hey: what's dis shit you're givin' me?

— Ain't shit... I ain't slept yet.

— So I hear.

I wash my hands. The knuckles sting under the cold water but I like that feelin'. The cold burns. Just burns away everythin' there. But then days weeks later a scratch appears. A scar that only I know about. Like a mark from a thing thass been an' gone an' leaves a trace. A definite thing. Shitsky just crowds me. I'm all set to ask him what the fuck he's starin' at.

— I hear Koom an' li'l Joey got beat op at dis ting.

— Yeah?

— Dat's what I hear.

— Who d'y'hear tha' off?

Shitsky just stands there like he ain't about to sing like a cuntprick canary. Fair enough. I wipe on a towel.

— Well if they got beat up they had it comin'. Na mean.

I'm tryina figure the chain of calls across town to get the facts into Shitsky's mouth in time for his mornin' game. I wait for him to shift his ass. But he don't. Just lounges there noddin' lookin' me over an' smoothin' down his zapata tache.

— Big talk ain' it?

— Beats small talk innit.

— Listen bod you are face to face with a guy who got *awards* for talking big. Orright? Yeah man I been round playin' d'fokkin world know'm sayin'. Talkin' big and coked to d'fokkin eyeballs. My *cohones* got so big with coke and talk and stars in my fokkin eyes they needed extra road crew for d'load. You hear me? We played gigs in one horse towns in Mexico an' in like the biggest fokkin stadium shit man in front of like *t'ousands* an'-

— So wha' y'tryina say?

Shitsky takes a step back an' slaps the palm of one hand with the back of the other. So I slouch.

— *What am I tryin' to say?* I'm givin' you my fokkin translation of d'fokkin' bible. I'm sayin' I know where d'fokk it's at. Yeah dat's right chief. Ok so let os be calm bigshot. Where d'fokk was I?... Ok. See I'm sayin' we played some gig one time an' der is dese dudes in d'support. Dey's all supposed to be *real* tight. Like dey ain't kissin' each other goodnight but dey is supposed to be down *tight*. Ok? Cos' dey is all makin' it. Dey's goin' op in d'world you know'm sayin'. But what are dey all doing? I tell you: fokkin each other op for *frontman status*. Right? Like dey's grabbin' the mikes out each odder's mouses man. Cuttin' cables with their teeth to fokk their boddy's solo riff in d'limelight whatever. *Stealin'* each odder's number one pussy. Now all dat: it just ain't right... See'm sayin?

Shitsky shrugs. I guess they don't call him Shitsky for nothin'. He stands with his palms out holdin' the shrug til I have to react.

— So?

— So? You askin' so? What you askin' me? What d'fokk am I talkin' for if you's ignorin' real fokkin wisdom. Word gets round you's ignorant of where it's at you's fokked. And where it's at is a little fokkin support for *your people*. Who you gonna turn to when d'fokkin *t'underbolt* strike you? What you gonna do?

— Have a kitkat, I say in his face.

I can see he ain't psyched up for backchat. So while he's lettin' it sink in I lean in for another go.

— *Skin op a li'l bod an get real bozzed.*

His face starts kinda expandin' with the angry heat inside of him. When he finally speak it's all choked up.

— You talk to me like dis? What d'fokk... You big now? All growed op? With Big Daddy Noodle in your ass or what?

I let him have the last word. Like I give a fuck. My people my ass. For a second I thought he knew somethin' about Koom. But Shitsky don't even know the beginnin' of his sentence. He just likes to talk big by tellin' people how they shouldn't talk big.

— ...I'm tryin' to say some shit to you that mean shit. See you just don't walk over your friends when shit's goin' down. With me? Whatever is your game and der is games believe me you ain't seen shit general. Know'm sayin'? So whatever. Know'm sayin'? An' I ain't sayin' I know shit you understand but... you's too young for all that *attitude*. Right? Friends is friends. Ok?

— Well tha' clears the air innit.

I brush past him an' go back toward the kitchen. In the corridor is a loada gig snaps of the Shitsky band in shiny purple jumpsuit shit. *Hey: dey's de heydays man...* He follows like before pictures knockin' still yackin'. We get back to the kitchen.

— What you tokkin about *clears the air*? What you mean dey *had it comin*? Dey's regular type o' guys an' you know it.

— So they pro'ly go' a regular type of beatin'.

— Fokk...

— Whassis? says Nood juttin' his neck out.

Any talk of violence gets Nood interested. It's his special topic an' apart from tick lists an' phone numbers it's the only thing he got memory for.

— Bad fokkin shit..., says Shitsky shakin' his head.

But violence gets all of us interested if truth be told. No matter if it's small or pumped up. Time stops an' you just wanna listen to the thing from beginning to end takin' in every last detail while the kettle screams an' zombies come down the chimney. But you just don't wanna sit face up with whoever's tellin' it. It's ok as long as it's tvstyle. Like you can shag in front of a victim an' feel nothin'.

— So whassi' 'bou' then? goes Nood.

Shitsky keeps stumm so I say:

— The Greek brothers got stuffed at the rave.

— Yeah well, says Nood blowin' through his nose, thass wha'appens when y'don't sor' y'tick. Innit?

Nood laughs an' I nod agreein' which I guess is what I'm there for. The rock stars're startin' to sweat serious now an' Nood loves it. He raises his eyebrows lookin' at Shitsky like he's invitin' him to talk back an' raise the stakes with each word.

— What's dis? What you sayin' Nood? C'mon man. I mean what-

Nood jumps up knockin' an empty mug spoon an' not so empty ashtray to the floor. His face is all screwed. He's had a late rush of whizz.

— I'm sayin' issall abou' laughter innit. I'm sayin' let the good fuckin' times roll. I'm sayin' I'm ge'in married at five an' tomorrow's tomorrow. Na mean.

They all look at each other in turn none of 'em givin' nothin' away. But on the other hand none of 'em can figure what the fuck to add that would bring the situation under control. Then Shitsky loses it.

— Now what d'fokk *you* tokkin about Nood? I mean what's dis *tomorrow's tomorrow* shit?

— Forget i' man, says Nood ballsin' gear an' bills. Just bring the sax...

Nine fifty

Go north to Hoxton where Nood gets his eel pie an' mash for breakfast. He says it's traditional like a *roots an' culture* thing. I tell him regular that some roots an' culture don't do nothin' 'cept stink up the fuckin' yard. Not to mention givin' the car a seafood rinse all the fuckin' way down Bethnal Green Road an' across Spitalfields. Down Brick Lane I park up to get *my* breakfast. On the street it's heavy incense curry spice an' a pockmarked cabbie beefin' to his flatcap pals about fares:

— ...They was all *German* so I told 'em I said if we're drivin' in circles it's cos *you* made us change the road signs...

Beyond them's the bakery stacked with bagels an' rolls an' pies just ready to go. As I'm goin' in for my cream cheese bagels an' apple pie which has come to be my all-time staple some sadfuck busker who couldn't find a tube station starts in with his sadfuck act. He's one of these crew cut army surplus travellin' folk hero assholes bringin' his music to the people all on his own like the revolution had gone on holiday an' left him behind.

— *Let me take you by the hand and lead you through the streets of London...*

Inside warm bread smells take a hold of me. I feel like crashin' right there on the floor to the sound of orders comin' in an' bakin' trays scrapin' an' the stomachs of the good the bad an' the seriously needy rumblin' with satisfaction. This is a typea place you can like an' keep likin' an' even when you're a million miles away it keeps you goin' just thinkin' 'bout it. Cos it's all about pleasure in a set-up like this.

I come out with my little bags of food all psyched up to chow down. But lyin' in a heap on the floor is the busker with eel pie in his gums an' the strings of his *king of the blues* guitar wirin' out all over. Nood's sittin' in the car with his arms folded an' the tecno blarin'. Out on the street people're stood starin'. I feel a lynch mob formin' in their minds. So we get the fuck out of there before I can eat.

Around ten thirty

We're drivin' east toward Victoria Park. Then left up Mare Street with grey dust risin' in the heat an' people pushin' prams never gettin' nowhere. Mare Street you can walk for days an' get nowhere. You ask someone where the fuck you are an' they tell you:

— *Sorry I was about to ask you the same thing.*

An' if you pick someone who's loaded down both hands with shoppin' an' must be goin' home an' ask them the same they tell you:

— *Sorry don't live round here.*

Some neighbourhoods're like that. You couldn't get a resident to confess they lived there if you held their babies to ransom. So we jump in the backstreets. London Fields to Hackney Downs. It's gettin' near breaktime an' thass the area Nood does school rounds. With Shitsky comin' up short things ain't lookin' good for him an' he's hungry for orders. We locate the first street an' I turn off the tape. Nood signals to slow down.

— Left by them railings. Do a li'l drive-by...

We go past an' look at the cars an' any types of people passin'. No mothers teachers vigilante pensioners. No crusaders or *community liaison*. Nothin'. Just sun splash. Very quiet. Remember walkin' through corridors at school while everyone was in lessons. All deserted an' that. Just silent distant. Weightless.

— Luvly jubbly... Turn i' round so's they can see my face an' stop up near tha' wall where i' says *Paddy Clark is a cunt...*

Wheel it round beneath a tree for the shade. We're across the street from the school gate. There's an ice-cream van parked up outside ready for business. So is Nood.

— Nice one, he says takin' out his cigs.

I stretch in the seat listenin' for a second to the engine clickin' coolin'. Unwrap a bagel an' take a big bite fillin' my mouth. The dough's still warm. The first taste brings back an old story.

— At school, I say chewin' hard, there was this skinnyass jewish kid Isaacs...

Nood lights a cig leans back on the headrest an' stares 'cross the street.

— ...He used to get two bagels off his mum every day for lunch. Only come lunch some ten ton scum called Blower used to grab the bagels off of him. Only Blower never ate them cos he only ever ate chips. Wha' he did righ' he just opened up the bagels one a' a time an' *licked* out the cream cheese. You get me? Then he closed 'em up an' passed 'em back to Isaacs. Only course the kid couldn't even look at 'em no more. Everyone sor'a felt sympathe'ic for Isaacs cos we all thought it was gross. Bu' there you go. I mean fifty other victims was talkin' up how Blower was gonna get stabbed. Bu' like who was gonna move on him? So this thing with Isaacs goes on untold times til one mornin' Isaacs come straigh' up to me an' give me his bagels. Just like that. So I'm like: *whass goin' on*? An Isaacs says well since he ain't gonna get to eat the thing when he wants I migh' as well. So I do. Logical thing. Y'na mean. Anyway come lunch Blower's grabbin' for the bagels bu' by then Isaacs ain't got 'em. Nor have I come to that cos my guts is already breakin' 'em down for poo. Bu' I ain't abou' to tell *fatboy*. Blower knows he's been thrown a curve an' tells Isaacs he's gonna make him piss blood. Slaps him up

43

shoves him against a wall an' moves in for the kill. Bu' just when we's all thinkin' Isaacs gonna get wasted he sor'a jumps forward practically into Blower's arms an' *licks* Blower righ' across his mug. Tellin' y'Blower turns *green*. Like he's fucked up infected. Like the doctor's just told him he's got three weeks. *If he's lucky*. His whole point o' view changes man. *Forever*. I swear I never seen Blower munch on anythin' again. Drops like... *stones*. Wastes away day by day hour by hour. Na mean. Meanwhile Isaacs man he's *sussed*: he gets *fat*. So fat one day he come to look just like Blower.

— Yeah? says Nood lookin' up. How come?

— Cos after that the people brung Isaacs deli the whole time na mean. To his *feet*. Na mean. Ain't *nobody* riskin' that facelick.

Nood smiles.

— How come you ain't told me tha' before Tax?

I put the last bit of bagel in my mouth thinkin' of an answer. But then a crowd of kids is comin' out the buildings an' splittin' off into their little posses. Some of them head for the ice-cream van. There's a group of real laggers lookin' all over like they're checkin' the coast. Among them are a coupla fourth years in baseball caps ten sizes too big an' angled like some LA streetgang.

Soon's they spot the car they start comin' straight toward us. But between them an' us is these girls buyin' ice-creams. The girls're all in their own crew gear with their wide laces an' logo tops an' bomber jackets with *RUDE* studded on the backs. They get their ice-creams but by then things've moved fast. The two caps're on 'em. Course they just have to do it. Like they was robots. Don't see their precise technique. Guess nobody does. All I do see is the tops of the girls' ice-creams spray white an' pink in the air catchin' sunligh'. Before fannin' ou' an' fallin' like sweet rain. Everyone stops a second to look. Then untold hell breaks out.

— You FUCKIN' SPUNKERS. Wankaaaahs.

— FISHCUNTS. Bitches.

Then they all take deep breaths an' start chantin' the same thing at each other.

— Yer mum yer mum yer mum....

The caps break off down the street toward us. Nood shakes his head.

— They don't know fuck abou' discretion innit Tax.

— Tell me man. One day they'll do us righ' here. How'm I gonna tell everyone I got busted for two quid an' a cornetto?

— Hey. Here they come.

The caps move in together boppin' an' shamblin' along with their bodies turnin' one way an' their heads another.

— Alrigh' man, says one with baggy pants an' no belt like he come straight from the cell.

— Nuff respec', says the other slouchin' over the car.

— What was you after?

— Es an' some rocky hash, says Baggy.

— Liked the last ones did ya?

— Wicked man, says Slouch. Go'a wai' for Shabs. He'll sor' ya na'm sayin?

— Shabs is safe. How many was you wantin'?

— Ten... An' a q.

— Ten?... Ten? Thass gonna cost na mean, goes Nood real pleased.

— Safe man. Shabs go' i'.

An' there's Shabs: pintsize MC Bigshot movin' slow an' wide across the street.

— Shabba's comin', says Shabs an' squats down by Nood's door so's I can hardly see him.

— 'Righ' Shabs how y'doin'? says Nood stickin' his fist out.

— Nuff respec', says Shabs bangin' an' slappin' Nood's fist accordin' to codes only Shabs could know.

Nood pulls a bag from down under an' counts out the Es in his lap.

— There's ten in there. An' a q. Thass one fifty an' thirty for the q. Who're the heavies Shabs?

Nood grins. Shabs nods to himself smilin' while Slouch an' Baggy lose their cool by the second shiftin' round nervous. Then Shabs disappears altogether behind the door. Second later his hand comes in over with one eighty of used up notes that you just know is up front dough from kids that's never gonna make it onto a tick list their whole ready cooked lives.

Nood passes out the magic bag. The caps're still itchy. Shabs grins an' says so's everyone can hear:

— Why? Dey make me look foolish?

— We ain't done nuthin' Shabs, say the heavies as one an' a little too rehearsed for their own good.

— *We ain't done nuthin' Shabs*, Shabs mimicks.

— They're alrigh', says Nood.

Shabs grins.

— Ma homies na mean.

— Ravin' are y'Shabs?

— Every day every night boy.

— Say no to drugs.

— Safe.

— Wicked. Alrigh' Tax...

Two streets away it's the same routine only when they ask for rocky Nood sells 'em car tyre from Bradford that smells worse than the eel. Supply of that's always handy. Some people like it.

Goin' on seventeen an' a half to eleven

So then we're backroadin' up to Stoke Newington through one of them ordinary residential streets when hundred feet away Nood spies a whore.

— Well heat me up... Innit.

I don't answer. She's leanin' against corrugated iron that fences off some boarded home. It's like no sooner you board up some place than the whole strip opens for business. This one's sor'a young sor'a scraggy an' sor'a blond in cut down jeans an' a t-shirt.

— Come on pull over man, he says grabbin' at the wheel.

So I just have to let go an' abandon control. Nood aims for a space but steers into the pavement doin' ten feet of kerbscrape til we're almost alongside of her. She looks young an' shy. In another life she's waitin' for her boyfriend. But I guess her story's in the worn out blue stilettos sweaty makeup an' red marks on her bare legs. Nood's checkin' her out. I'm checkin' him.

— Y'ain't serious. Wha' the fuck y'gonna do?

— This is my last chance Tax, says Nood lookin' for dough.

Nood's hand movin' to his pocket is her cue. Arms folded she shakes her hair an' starts steppin' over with her *sassy as a breeze* act.

— I don't believe it.

— Iss my last fuckin' chance I'm tellin' ya.

— I don't believe it.

— Whassama'er man I go'a do i'. My nature's callin'. This is it. My last chance na mean.

— I still don't believe it...

— Fuck's with you Tax?

— Ain't *necessarily* your last chance is it?

Nood stops searchin' an' looks at me like the penny's workin' its way through to his brain. Which it ain't no secret to say is in two small parts somewhere in his underpants. By that time she's bendin' down an' lookin' in the car. Screwy little eyes. Her nose is sniffly. So she sniffs. Nood looks at her an' sniffs back. She smiles at him.

— You got a summer cold as well?

Summer cold my ass. Nood don't answer. He just smile back in her face.

— Save it man. 'Sides time is money righ' now, I'm urgin' thinkin' more about her than him.

— Yeah maybe, he says examinin' the feel of his money. I ain't thunk it through like that before na mean. Ain't *necessarily* my last chance is it. I'm free. I'm free by law innit. Weddin' or no. I'm a man na mean. I do things in my *own* time. In my *own* way. I draw my *own* conclusions.

— So whassall tha' then, she sniffs, a yes or a no?

Nood turns back to her. This is surely my cue to stick the car in gear which I do but not quick enough.

— You givin' me pressure? Wha'? You one of them teenage crack whores I bin readin' about? You should-

She just throws a half dozen good kicks at the car door with them blue stilettos as we pull away. Nood leans well out the window.

— *You* should be chasin' mechanical rabbits. Na mean, he shouts.

He looks at me for applause. Life's light entertainment to him. Like he's doin' his own stand-up show with a canned audience laughin' cryin' screamin' out for more. He don't care 'bout nothin' else. Anythin' else come second. If that. How did he come to love himself? And the sound of his own laughter. But chasin' laughs he leaves a trail of waste.

Near the hour

Still grinnin' Nood directs me over to the last school on the
round. A drive-by down Newington Green. This time we
park up fifty feet away from the gate cos there's a lo'a busy
people loafin' round.

Some ex fifth year called Snipper on account of the
dotted line an' scissors tattooed on his neck clocks us
passin'. He lumbers out from a playground where he ain't
s'posed to be to meet us. He's six foot plus with plooks
bustin' out his face an' mouth an' a seriously disturbed
look like his mum breastfed him battery acid. Then there's
his fucked up dog that chews through cars called The Law.
Need a fuckin' elephant gun for both of them. But they
keep the school under control an' the teachers don't fuck
with 'em.

Snipper sticks his pus mug in through the window.

— Alrigh' Nood, he says tryina whisper which for
medical reasons he cannot.

The Law's bitin' an' scratchin' his way into the car.

— No i' ain't as i' goes, says Nood. Got a little job for
you. There's some fourth year called Turner an' he's-

— I'll deal with the fucker's case. I'll punish 'im. Put The
Law on 'im. Bite his fuckin' balls off. Whass 'e done?

— Been sellin' gear innit. Ain't figured out yet...

— Yeah yeah.

— ...who he's been gettin' i' off...

— Yeah yeah.

— ...Don't break him or nothin' righ'.

— Yeah y-

— Snips you lissnin'?

— Yeah yeah.

— I just wanna know where-

— Solid. Solid. He'll gimme names. Solid Nood.

— Better fuckin' be Snipper cos I don't want you bustin' in the classroom like before. Righ'? *Righ'*?

— Wha'f I do?

— I said no... They'll have you back with that dickhead.

— They take you on holiday these days. Ain't you heard?

— I know bu' I need you on patrol. I just wanna know who the li'l cunt's scorin' off of.

Nood passes out a magic bag an' Snipper sorts him out with four crisp fifties. Whatever else he's reliable.

— Ge' us any crack?

— Could do... but I ain't gonna.

— Fuckin' business out there for grabs Nood. Pissar'ist yardie kids goin' for it. I need the fuckin' wash rock yeah. Wha' y'gonna do?

— I'll make my move when I'm ready, says Nood like Vito from Vegas.

I get wind of this unmarked Astra parkin' up down the street an' tap Nood. Snipper splits the other way an' we ease back onto the road headin' up to the Astra.

— Look a' them muggy boneheads.

— Don't look a' them Nood you give 'em heart attack.

They're already sunk down in their seats an' breakin' out snacks like they're on a long job. They eye us over as we pass givin' us a long kinda sneerin' *whose turf are you on* look. Whole thing's like in slowmo. They both got packets of pork scratchings. Nice. An' they both know for sure what we're about.

— Too lazy to do fuck the pair of 'em, Nood mutters.

— Tha' or they got their earners.

I keep lookin' in the rearview in case they get a sudden rush of law enforcement. But they fade off quiet an' we're back with the flow tryina concentrate on the schedule.

Eleven twenty

Nood builds a fat blunt with some pers skunk an' we have a smoke to celebrate the shells we pulled in. Not that it's gonna be enough. We're movin' down Green Lanes the land of triple-parked beemers where parkin' law don't count an' old guys in shirts play dominos on fold-out tables tryina to keep their fresh cleaned shoes out the aubergine an' chilli mashed on the pavement.

Then some dippy blouse in a Volvo in front gets up my nose cos of the way she hits the brakes whenever a car comes down the opposite lane. Nood notices her an' his face changes. He takes these things worse'n me. She almost stops in the middle of the road for nothin'.

— I don't fuckin' believe i'. See tha' Tax. She can't even... Fuckin' look at i' the fa' fuckin'-... Doin' i' again. Fa' fuckin' slag. Do 'er Tax.... Go on man give her a bit of side impact na mean.

She starts off again real slow. We're followin' behind stoppin' an' startin' with the skunk turnin' my head to elastic. She clocks us in the rearview. Can tell by the angle of her head. The way her shoulder shifts. We're all the way up Green Lanes Nood punchin' his knee before she finally turns off onto the Harringay ladder an' puts her foot down like she's tryina get away. You can tell from her drivin' exactly how she's feelin'. Without thinkin' I turn off behind an' follow a foot from her bumper now flashin' an' hootin'

53

up the hill. Me Nood an' the car are one. Just one thing. One instinct. One thing thass gonna make a difference. We keep up the pressure til she swerves off into a driveway.

We roll past. Can't see her eyes through her big dippy shades. Nood gets off on it though.

— Wicked. Leas' we know where she lives innit Tax. Come back in a coupla days. Where the fuck are we?

— Near Turnpike Lane or so.

— Y'jokin'. Go'a go all the way back down Holloway to Kingsley's then over to Marcello's bar an' I go'a sign at three then get home an' change an' that an'...

Nood's mobile goes which saves my earhole.

— Alrigh' babes. Owsi' lookin' your end?.... Yeah?.... Stell.... babes.... Ste-.... I'm-.... babes list-.... I'm fuckin' tellin' ya issunda control. Alrigh'? Alrigh'? I'll fuckin' do it I told ya.... No no babes I go'a keep this line open na mean.... La'er babes.... Yeah alright. La'ers.

Nood's well pissed off. He sparks up a fag jams the tape back on an' sorts us out some sulph which is this twenny a gee ramraider guaranteed to bring relatives back from the dead. I just swallow it down in a rizla. Nood shakes his head.

— Been bonin' the bitch three years man: she knows the score na mean an' she's talkin' charlie an' Es over the airwaves. An' listen to this: we go'a pick up her mum from Harlesden.

— Oh wha'?... *Wha?*

— Na mean.

— When?

— In a jiffy.

— Fucksat mean in a jiffy?

— Last thing before the town hall.

— Well leas' it ain't now man. Couldna faced nobody's mother now.

The tape seems to bring on the whizz so we're canin' it down Tollington to Holloway avoidin' cones an' vans with

my heart always ten feet in front of the car. I'm grindin'
down my teeth an' gibberin' shit.

— How's Stell an' y'mum an' sister gettin' down. Y'go' go
separate innit I mean do we gots to go get them as well or
wha'? I mean who-

— Lendon.

— Lendon Lendon. As in- You're off y'tree Nood. Off y'...
I mean Lend's gonna pull pigs from all over the fuckin'
North Circ.

Lendon's white beemer with tinted windows would be
enough for most cops. But with *The Punisher* sprayed
across the side in pink he's takin' the piss. I'm thinkin' if
he's ever gonna make it down Euston Road to the town
hall. Cos if he didn't we'd be barrowin' Stell's mum around
all day lookin' for 'em in every-

— Park up park up park up.

— Eh? Sorry man yeah.

Go past the second-hand furniture shop an' turn off
Holloway onto Liverpool Road. Park up in a side street
lookin' round for wardens. We scan about lazy keepin'
ourself casual as we make toward Kingsley's. That stretch
of Holloway's alright with its old busted shops. Mouldy
fridges on the street. Shops that've given up on cleanin'
their windows. It's got heart. Somewhere. It's also got pink
tits. Nood's seen 'em too on a creased up magazine cover
just lyin' on the grey dark pavement.

His eyes follow a trail of covers to the porn stall further
up the road. A sweaty furniture man's sat nearby with his
junk goods his face red an' polluted in the sun an' exhaust.
He follows Nood's eyeline an' grins an' winks at him. But
Nood like the rest of Holloway Road never stops to wink
back. He just goes direct to the stall which is a splintered
up cart. He's already pickin' out a magazine an' kinda
moanin' as I join him.

— Gaargh... Bitch...

— Take it you like her Nood.

Nood pulls out a cardboard box of used up mags an' looks round for the stallholder. There's this old geezer in a brown sor'a cowboy suit with tassles sat on a crate surrounded by piles of mags an' scummy books. He's thumbin' through one of his mags lookin' at the pictures an' chucklin' to himself like he was flippin' through a family album an' seein' old faces.

— How much for the box mate?

The old cowboy don't even look up from his memories.

— For- forty pee for one or two pou- pound the box. Ple-plenty o' cunt in there mate.

— Wha' y'want with the box man, I say to Nood confidential.

— For the paper na mean.... Cut up the charlie la'er.

— You don't wanna go puttin' kuf in there man. Geezers like him have been creamin' over it for-

— Nah be alrigh'. Oi mate: Here's a coupla squids for the box alrigh'.

— Y- you'll be w- w- well away with those 'uns mate. Ple-plenty o' cunt in there. Plenty.

— Nice one. We'll be back for the box in a li'l while ok. You better not stiff us old man...

Nood creases up.

— Hey d'ya get it Tax?

— Yeah Nood.

— The porn merchant better not stiff us.... Wicked.

So Nood's in a better frame of mind as we get to Kingsley's half a dozen doors up.

Gone twelve

The sign in Kingsley's cosmetics an' weddin' business —
*Partners In Cream: we'll make you look good for any
occasion* — hangs above this funeral parlour an' when
weddings dried up for a time cos of one recession thing or
other all Kingsley had to do was go downstairs. The door's
buzzed. We go up.

The office is one mega space. One corner's stacked up
with creams for the face an' make-up. On the far side's a
photo studio with lights an' cameras an' metal stands an'
cables everywhere. Kingsley's partner Baba is gettin' some
woman into position in front of a screen with a whole
library of books an' shit painted on it. This woman's
wearin' a black gown an' hat like a professor an' she's
holdin' some fancy frilled up certificate you couldna never
thought of in a million years. But for me the killer's right
there on the main wall: a monster fuckin' photograph of
Nood holdin' Mac against a dark blue background. They're
lookin' into each other's eyes like they was strangers in the
night.

Kingsley's blabbin' an' laughin' on the phone while he's
fixin' his hair in front of a mirror on his desk. He grins an'
waves at us to sit down.

— Just book in.... Sure book in.... You can have that or
I've got a University of East Basingstoke here if you want.

Same difference in LA. Know'm saying? Certainly can. We do all of that sir and so much more.... Alright ok sure call me when you know.

Kingsley hangs up an' spins round on his chair.

— Lookin' smoov Kings.

— Feeling smoothe Nood. How things Tax?

— Kickin'.

— Big day right Nood? I've arranged a guy for the video so he's coming down with us ok. Expecting some foxy ladies at the reception cos my prime's at stake. Know'm saying? You guys want a coffee?

We don't mind so Kingsley punches out some styrofoam coffees from a vendin' machine an' passes them round.

— So who's on the 'A' list tonight?

— Well Stell's invitin'-

— I was thinking more along the line of *rare imports*, says Kingsley touchin' up the sides of his hair. Thing is I could have had two types of pussy tonight. I just financed new wheels and I mean why shell out for a passenger-side air bag... You know?

— Don't worry Kings, says Nood, no way you're gonna be disappointed.

— Better not be..., goes Kingsley leanin' back an' lookin' at Nood eyes all twinkly. So twinkly in fact that I sometimes think he's wearin' specs.

—...Because the thing is... I'm passing up two *serious dangermuffs* and they're both called Cameel. Well actually one's Camilla and the other's K'meel with an apostrophe.

— Whassa'? says Nood.

Kings looks at me like the whole thing's obvious then back at Nood like it ain't.

— It's the way she spells her name man. She more or less read me the instruction manual that came with it. '*K*', she says looking deep in to my eyes, *is an ancient symbol of fertility*. What as in *Kingsley* I say... But she was not amused...

Kingsley laughs at his own joke an' pulls his crisp white cuffs down one at a time. Nood's about to say somethin' but Kings waves a manicured finger at him clearin' his throat.

— Then she goes: *And the apostrophe represents the sperm entering the unspoken mystery of womanhood... Wow* I exclaim somewhat blown away. I mean don't get me wrong guys I love that kind of talk and by now I'm all over her. So what's *meel*? I enquire. And you know what she says? She goes: *That's what you're buying me tonight.*

Kingsley shakes his head an' takes a sip of coffee. The phone rings.

— Don't you just hate smart pussy?

— I wouldn't know, says Nood.

Kingsley grins lifts the receiver an' talks bollocks down it for a coupla minutes til Baba's finishin' up with the professor. After she's gone Baba loosens his tie locks up an' comes over.

— Guys...

We all shake. Baba's hands're the size of fryin' pans. An' at six six the rest of him ain't ryvita. When he sits his swivel chair disappears from view so's it looks like he's sittin' in the air. Serious fuckin' guy.

He pushes a little bag of kuf over the desk an' Kingsley starts rackin' up lines on his mirror. We're all chillin' an' it looks like it's gonna be *have a nice day* kinda business. Then of course Nood's mobile goes. He's a cunt like that. He tries to whisper into the mouthpiece even though there's fuck all point.

— ....Yeah.... Yeah look babes I can't talk now... Cos I'm in a meetin'.... Babes I'm gonna-.... Well jus-.... Well just get a loada extra sausages then....

I can feel Baba lookin' us over.

— ...I don't know any fuckin' vegetarians... Well they can have the spuds then innit.

Nood switches off gesturin' helpless. Baba's scratchin' his little beard an' still lookin'.

— Look at the pair of you. Your garms are wacked. You're a dog's dinner.

— Just one? I say.

Kingsley an' me laugh. Nood shifts in his chair. He ain't too sweet on personal criticism. Specially from Baba.

— Been on the go na mean Baba. Like we been blowin' up all over innit Tax.

— Is righ', I echo.

— They're gonna transform by five, says Kingsley.

— Yeah? Well they'll need the whole fuckin' stockroom of creams to do it.

Baba laughs his forty a day laugh so me an' Nood fix up a grin an' scratch our mugs at the same time. We watch Kingsley roll up a fifty. He snorts up a coupla lines like he means it an' passes the mirror to me as he starts sniffin'. With Baba checkin' me out I snort up my lines at least as loud as Kings an' pass to Nood. Then Nood snorts his hard as he can as I'm sniffin' an' Baba snorts up his even louder as Nood's sniffin' an' by the time the mirror gets back to Kingsley everyone's tryina snort an' sniff louder than everyone else. The rush hits Nood first.

— Pukka gear pukka fuckin' gear. Gi's a P on twenny how much you got?

— How much do you owe us?

— Kings you know I'll sor' ya after today. I'm waitin' on–

— You know the score after today? says Baba.

— Hundre' per cent man na mean. Safe. Nothin' to worry abou'.

— Lord have mercy.

— Kings I'm on the case. Pukka fuckin' gear. One line of this an' everyone looks like they're wearin' suspenders y'na mean.

But ain't none of us rollin' with this point of view. Not now. Baba don't bat an eye.

— You know the score, he says.

— The score yeah... Wha' abou' it?

— You know it right?
— The score. Yeah. I know that.
— Cos what's the opposite?
Nood shoots a look at me then looks back at Baba.
— Wha'?
— The opposite of what you just said.
— The opposite.
— What's the exact opposite?
There's this silence for like a second an' Nood's tryina figure the right answer. Kingsley's got his head down thumbin' some papers on his desk an' I'm tryina look into space that's nowhere in particular but wherever it ain't at Baba.
— The exact opposi' you mean?
— That's what I asked yes the exact opposite of what you said.
— Of wha' *I* said?
— When I asked you if you knew the score you said yeah you did. Right?
— Yeah right.
— So what's the exact opposite?
— Look man there ain't nothin' to worry-
— Is that the exact opposite of what you said?
— ...I'll sort it... I said-
— *That's* the exact opposite? That's not the exact opposite.
— Well wha' is then?
— Now you're asking me.
Baba's gettin' steamed up. He pulls on his beard. All the time I'm thinkin' no way's he gonna fuck Nood up on his weddin' day. But you just don't know what's in the mother's head. I catch Kingsley's eye a second.
— Are you listening? I'm asking you what's the opposite the exact opposite of what you said when you-
— Baba... Give him a break...
Kingsley grins at Nood.

— ...The guy's big day. He's on the case. He says he'll sort
it. And he will.

— I will. I know I will. I know the score.

Quarter to one

Even after that horseshit Nood squeezes ten gees on tick tellin' them he'll shift it by tomorrow. My head's reelin' as I carry the box of porn to the boot. Everythin's pilin' up. Nood's gonna have to start sellin' the gear to Stell's mum to make inroads. Bein' round him now's like havin' Baba sittin' on my face tellin' jokes. We set off down Liverpool Road. Do a right an' sift over Caledonian to York Way almost gettin' mashed by this awesome eighteen wheeler pullin' out of a concealed entrance. Nood don't even notice. His phone goes.

— Yeah?... Yeah... Yeah Lendon I know all that. Them's the travel arrangements... Yeah... So wha' the fuck you phonin' for?...

Nood passes over the phone.

— Wants a word...

— Yo blood whassup? I say puttin' it on.

— *Yeah lissen Tax,* Lendon rushes, *Nood's signin' round three yeah. Need a word with you. Go'a discuss one or two things na mean. In that sidestreet. You know the one...*

— Sure sure Lend, I say aware of Nood, that be swell.

I switch off passin' back the phone.

— Wha' d'he want?

— Says his sister'll be there.

— Wha' an' he's go'a tell *you* that?

— Easy man. I was sweet on her way back innit.

— I heard tha' off you before, says Nood smilin'. An' it wasn't so way back.

— Maybe.

Turn right onto Agar Grove an' steam down toward the bridge with the sun dancin' through the trees. I'm tryina predict the subject Lendon's go'a discuss with me. It might be Nood who's gettin' wed but he ain't the only one sweatin' about it. It's like I can feel Nood's weddin' is about to shift a gear in a loada people's lives.

Almost under the rail bridge is the Pink Goose with a tree growin' near 'nough out its side that one day's gonna bring the whole place down. Unless the tough bastard weeds growin' out front decide to eat the place for snacks first. Nood's deep in thought or somethin' so I pull up hard right outside the bar just to spark him a bit. But he bangs his skull on the dash.

— Cunt.

— Sorry man. Wan' an aspirin?

But Nood's already out the car massagin' his head.

— Ay... Not too soon you arrive...

I grin out the window at Marcello. He's sittin' on the step of the Goose in his apron smokin' down a juicy bud sun on his scratchy face. Like the work was done an' the good times'd come. Or somethin'.

— Got held up at Kingsley's na mean, I say gettin' out.

— I hear you... De bastard Baba start to talkin' you're fucked.

— Business firin' yeah? says Nood staggerin' round to the entrance.

— Fucky shit all de time Noo-dell.

Which ain't no surprise. There's a table with someone slumped over it sleepin' a cigarette still burnin' in his fingers. Old crusty flies're feastin' on a half-eaten cheese sandwich. Marcello's skanky dog stands pantin' its tongue off by a dustbin. Marcello heaves himself up wipin' his hands on the apron an' passin' Nood the spliff.

— So, he says slappin' Nood's back, de bigga day...

Nood winces an' stomps inside bangin' the door open with his fist. Marcello's kinda knocked back.

— What did Iya say? Ay Taxi what-

— Forget i'. Iss his big day.

— Dat's what Iya said... Dat's what Iya fucky said... Shit. Come troo to de kitchen.

So we go into the flaky steampit Marcello calls a café. Best thing about it is Marcello's sister Steffi. She reminds me of this woman in The Sting who works in a café only it turns out she's a mafia assassin. Which could be the case with Steffi cos she makes the direst fuckin' crapuccino in the north. I sit up by the bar while Nood gets shagged for his money in the kitchen.

— You look like you haven' sleep, says Steffi servin' one up.

An' she still looks asleep. Which is her whole vibe an' mostly why I like her.

— Don't judge the way I look sugar cos inside I'm the best man.

Steffi don't get this dumb line but smiles at me anyway as she shakes some chocolate-covered sand onto the sewage in my cup. Her black hair's all over the place an' she's chewin' gum with her mouth open like she don't care.

— So you comin' la'er?

She starts sortin' forks knives spoons into a divided tray her hands movin' so fast I can't keep up.

— I donno...

All the things I'm thinkin' of sayin' to her just get drowned by the clashin'.

— ...Issup to Marcello if he closes or no. I justa work here.

— Not much to close is there...

I look along the bar at the only punter. Fifty odd dyed blonde all hitched up in the afternoon like she's slack an'

on the pull. She looks over at me smilin' an' narrowin' her eyes.

— Have you got a light?

I must be dreamin'. Steffi flips her a matchbook. Miss Slack crosses her legs like she's gettin' ready for somethin'. She tears off a match an' strikes it away from her with a move like she was castin' loose change to the people. Then she lets the flame steady puts the cigarette in her pouty mouth looks all the way along it still fixin' me. Then she puts match to cigarette an' takes a long pull lookin' like she's just come in her knickers. She holds the smoke down then blows out the matchflame with a thin jet still lookin' at me so deep why I could fall in love. In the kitchen things're soundin' more like usual.

— I fuckin' told ya to shift the last lot. You still ain't sor'ed us for tha' innit. Now you want this gear on tick.

— Iyama tryi' to 'elp you out wid your pro'lem. You want to sheef tonight ok but de money come only tomorrow tomorrow.

— You dozy fuckin' cunt I'll get stuffed tomorrow.

— Ok no pro'lem.

— Issa fuckin' problem for me though innit.

— No. I 'ave idea...

The kitchen door closes an' I'm left lookin' at Steffi. Her stomach's sor'a pushin' against the bar stretchin' this little top over her nipples. She's wipin' saucers an' stackin' them. Wipin' an' stackin' an' wipin' an' stackin'. Every time she wipes the top stretches. Every time she stacks it kinda sags. I take a sip of the coffee hopin' a fly'll fall in it.

— What time Noodell is getti' married?

— Five but the do ain't til after. You got the invite innit? Slice of Heaven. Kilburn.

— Sure: Slice of de Heaven. I have friend who will work in dis place already and I think to may be to take a job too der also.

— Yeah?

— Yeah because here you know working with him I mean Marcello it is well like you know—

Steffi does a class impression of someone hangin' themself complete with suffocation noise.

— Y'na mean, I say forcin' a laugh. Well you go'a try an' come down. Cos everyone's comin' down. The whole nation. It'll be well...

But I dunno what it'll be. So I just say nice like an asshole.

— *Nice?* Only nice only?

— Thassa lot already Steff. Nah... Y'na mean it'll be a good crack. Friendly like a weddin'. People buryin' hatchets but not in people's backs. Na'm sayin'.

But Steffi ain't got a clue what I'm sayin'. Come to that neither do I. Get a loada guys together for a laugh an' someone's go'a get maimed. Probably me. Way it is. Steffi sticks a hair clip in her teeth an' pulls her hair back so's I see the lighter skin under her ear. I'm startin' to think Nood's takin' a long time which worries me cos it means Marcello's explainin' complicated shit.

One day I'm gonna kiss Steffi right there. Under her ear. There's laughs comin' out the kitchen. Me an' Steff exchange a look. Now whatever the idea it's gonna be real stoopid. Marcello ain't exactly an ideas man. He's a three time loser from Willesden who came to Camden like it was Miami. He tried to set up a pizza 'n' charlie delivery service called the northern line. Got the beat up van an' everythin'. But the asshole left it in the square mile with the blinkers on an' the gear inside. They blew it up in a controlled explosion. So his story goes. Nood swings out the kitchen.

— Less mo'or.

— Eh? Where we goin'?

— Issall in me 'ead. Alrigh' Steff? See y'all down there.

— Goo' luck Noodell.

Near two

Nood says to Swains Lane then fuck all else except for last minute hand signals. So I drive.

DOG DOG TSS DOGGA DOGGA DOG TSSS.

Cross the choked up Camden road an' down the back of Kentish Town spreadin' cyclists. Nood holds a wrap of coke open an' I do some dabs. Then charge up Highgate road at fifty as my whole gob turns to blubberschlubber. YAAAAAAH. Manage to stop at the Parliament Hill crossin' while a squad of schoolgirls marches over. The teacher stands in the middle of the road after they've crossed an' mouths a big poncey thank you expectin' a smile in return. Nood follows her gaze squintin'. He starts rollin' down the window. I push the pedal to the metal an' swerve round her. Save her life why not. My mind's mainly on what the fuck Nood cooked up in the kitchen of the Pink Goose.

Do a right into Swains Lane past the shops with their own resident lush lookin' like a black hole against the pukey colours of benetton people. We're screamin' along in third as it gets steeper an' steeper an' the trees get greener an' the gaffs bigger an' then I park up at a four storey gaff that Nood indicates. Lions on marble pillars. Guard dog warnings. Steel shutters. Alarms. Videos. Spotlights. Satellites. The works.

— So wha' we gonna do?

— The business na mean, says Nood straightface. Just bell Stell...

The business. Like fuck. I look up at this place. Like som'in out of Star Wars with a front door. The business... Nood lights up.

— Babes... Yeh yeh we're almost home now... Yeah alright see y'there if I don't see ya... Hey: whassa' racket?... Yeah? Well the girlsa go'a go cos I'm takin' a soak na mean... La'er babes.

So we're out the car up the steps an' Nood's ringin'. He dances from foot to foot pattin' his thigh to some beat or tokin' hard on his cigarette. He's still on the bell an' doin' his thing when the door opens. This pinkish sort of woman 'bout our age stands there holdin' her fringe out her face like she had a headache.

— Hello. Can I help you?

— Yes you can. Hello. I'm lookin' for Edward.

— ...Er... Right yes... Who shall I say is calling?

— Kingsley.

I start to sweat. I look aroun' an' I'm seein' dog faces in the bushes an' hotlines to private security firms. She shouts inside without movin' from the door.

— Edwaaard! D'ling there's a *Kingsi?* at the door...

We hear steps an' this pinkish sort of guy comes an' stands next to her. They look at us like we come to fix the toilet.

— We come about the charlie.

The guy twigs. His face goes radioactive with delight.

— Oh Kingsy! D'ling this is Kingsy the man I was telling you about. For the charlie cocaine... You sounded different on the phone.

— Bunged up wa'n' I.

— Oh I'm so sorry how rude of me I didn't even introduce myself I'm Gillian. This is Edward. Legal bods in the city both of us. Most days that is ha.

— Alrigh' Gillian?

Gillian don't look like she's ever answered that question before.

— Yes... Thank you...

— Look you'd better come in hadn't you? says Edward.

— We go'a come in. Not like we're floggin' dishcloths for the handicapped na mean. Usually have a cup o' tea.

— Oh... Right... Come in, says Gillian lookin' at Nood's fag like it was nuclear waste.

We step into the hall. Gillian rushes off holdin' her fringe an' we follow Edward in across the parquet him clackin' an' us squeakin' along. We go up an' down some little steps an' so on til we get to the lounge which ought to be in a fuckin' guide book. Can't see the flash wallpaper for the clapped out paintings of stark naked bodybuilder types with tiny balls like they done too much steroid. There's CDs records an' stereo gear by the yard. A bubbly fish tank with stuff swimmin' in it that you wouldn't want served up with chips. A baby grand piano with a music book open at *Twinkle twinkle little star.* An' Smart Eddie's in the middle of his antiseptic kingdom colour-coded in shades of brown. Now I know Nood's burglarised a coupla breezy yards in his time but even he's lost for words.

— Do sit down... Gillian'll get the tea in a minute.

I sink into this white sofa with satiny cushions til I'm sittin' like a spider with my knees above my head. Edward crosses his legs in an armchair with his fingertips joined under his chin an' Nood stands with arms folded gazin' round at the ornaments an' nick-nacks an' shit. Edward's followin' his eyes round the room wonderin' what to protect first.

— Appreciate you coming so promptly. Bit of a dinner do this evening. Old uni chum's finally bought a girl a ring. Not official yet. Not til next Nov. So tonight's a sort of inner circle pre-engagement pre-stag pre-*more or less everything* knees-up. I hope...

— I understand. How much of the charlie cocaine was you after?

Then Gillian comes clackin' back in with an ashtray. We all look at her. She takes her fringe out her face sees Nood's folded arms an' starts to get embarrassed.

— D'ling are you getting tea?

Gillian's fringe drops but I can see her eyes checkin' bowls an' flower pots.

— Yes... Yes I'm just putting it on... Back in a moment.

On the way out she's still glancin' about tryina figure what happened to the fag. Nood turns to me with a sort of *she'll never fuckin' find it* look on his face an' sits down next to me.

— I got twenny gees here. Do it for sixty a gee all the way through yeah? Twelve 'undred.

— Twelve... Ah. Oh. That's rather more than I had in mind, says Eddie gettin' more nervous.

— Iss only twenny gees Edward. You an' your chums'll spunk that in no time.

— It's fine. Fine. Really. Absolutely. Just that... Well you see...

Edward leans in lowerin' his voice but lickin' his lips like here comes a jokey secret.

— ...'er indoors might not approve...

— Yeah? Well I don't do house calls for a loada batwank. Busy schedulerooni na mean.

— I can quite appreciate that...

I still can't tell how Nood's plannin' on dealin' with this but there's ugliness round the corner. Once Nood's got someone he just toys with 'em. I suppose he spent too much time on his own as a kid grillin' insects with a magnifyin' glass.

Gillian brings the tea an' sticks the tray down in front of us. She unpacks the china on to the table an' moves a plate of biscuits a millimetre to let us know she pulled out all the stops. Then she tries lookin' at Edward to find out whass goin' down. Only he's too nervy to look back.

— Alright d'ling thanks. Would you mind waiting next door.

— You-

— Next door please darling this is business.

— But the-

— Next door thank you.

Edward tenses his face an' makes it go a bit red to let her know he's serious.

— Well... Help yourselves to tea. And biscuits, she says on the way out.

When she's gone Nood pours three cups takin' special care not to drip it on the carpet. He sort of plucks up the end of the pot as the tea reaches the right level in the cup. Edward's watchin' every move like Nood was figure-skatin'. Nood's hand hovers over the little silver milkpot.

— Milk an' sugar yeah?

— Just a smidgen of milk please thanks.

Nood nods slow like he handles smidgens fifty time a day. He takes the milkpot in his thumb an' forefinger pours an' plucks three times for each cup never spillin' nothin'. Then he reaches over to Edward with the cup an' saucer combo an' y'can't so much as hear a rattle.

— Thanks. Thanks very much. Great.

Nood heaps a coupla spoons of sugar in his own cup an' stirs so's the sugar grinds.

— Under circum circumstances I could consider doin' you half but I am pressed for time an' you must pay for the twenty.

— Sorry?

Nood passes round the biscuits.

— No. No thanks. Thank you... You see the thing is-

— No Edward. There's no thing right, says Nood lettin' the biscuit plate half drop back on the table.

Edward seems to gulp at the sight of the jumbled biscuits. Like his whole operation was suddenly slippin'.

— Well the thing is..., he starts awkward pro'ly expectin' Nood to fist in.

But Nood's tuckin' in to them biccies just eatin' one while checkin' out the next. So Edward looks at me but I'm busy tuckin' in too.

— ...Thing is... Or rather the whole story is..., says Edward startin' off again.

— Yeah go on, says Nood.

— ...Gee- Gillian that is- hasn't actually taken cocaine before and well... I- I just don't think we should overdo it. I mean that sort of quantity... it is quite a lot...

— Have you thought abou' stockpilin' for the new year? Or sellin' on for a tidy profit?

— No. No that I mean those possibilities hadn't crossed my mind, says Edward smoothin' creases on his trousers.

Nood picks on his teeth waitin' for Edward to look up from his trousers. When he does Edward's face is all grin. Even his body's all grin. A whole new body language.

— Oh well... I suppose we'll all end up like *lobotomised dwarfs* tonight...

He leaves his jaw hangin' ready to laugh with us. Only we don't.

— If that's menna be funny, goes Nood, iss in bad taste. You should never poke fun at them whass mashed up by life.

— No of course- God I've got nothing against dwarfs it's ju-

— You go'a sort us out innit, I say sippin' my tea.

— Yes of course but the thing you see-

— No, says Nood, I said there's no *thing* righ'.

— It's just a little-

— Even a little thing righ'.

— N'no you see I was about-

— NO... Righ'?

73

— I'm s'r'y I don't qui-

— NO... Righ'?

— Well-

— No. Righ'?

— Alright...

— Righ'. So sort us out then, says Nood takin' the bag of charlie out his trousers.

— Pukka fuckin' gear, I say.

— Yes I'm sure I'm sure but you see the thing is-

— Do 'im.

I look at Nood as I'm sippin' my tea not really believin' what he said. Everythin's clockworkin' along. Eddie's all set to cave in. I wanna point this out to him. But Nood's got other plans. He blanks me chompin' on a chocolate wafer type thing with his hand cupped under for the crumbs.

— ...Wha'?... Whassa'? I say under my breath.

— Do the cunt, says Nood crunchin' with dry bits of wafer stickin' on his lips.

I stop sippin' an' look at Edward slowly over the rim of the cup. I dunno why slowly. Like I'm expectin' him not to have heard. But he has. He half stands for no reason an' looks at me then Nood then me again.

So I stand up an' I'm lookin' at Nood then him then Nood again. An' he's lookin' at Nood then me then Nood. 'Ventually him an' me are lookin' at each other again. He sort of shrugs like he's sympathetic with me cos we're in the same boat an' don't really wanna scrap. But he don't see it's go'a be done now. I take a step toward him. First he's scared but he realises I don't know what I'm gonna do. So his shoulders seem to go back like he's gonna fight. Takes a deep breath. Even squints like he's tough. Then course Gillian has to come back in.

— More tea?

I take another step toward Edward an' spit in his face.

— My- I- What..., splutters Eddie.

— I'll take a grand, says Nood, seein' as how you're ravin' tonigh'. Na mean.

— Oh... my... god, says Gillian in little breaths. Are you... alright? D'ling?

Edward stands there with his hands close to his face but somehow he can't touch himself.

— Jus- yes... I think so. F- For god's sake get the- book.

Me an' Nood exchange a glance while Gillian searches in a panic for this book on one of the shelves.

— I can't remem- I mean- which is it I can't-

— Financial... something or other. Jurisprudence. Got it? Have you got it. Have you-

— No I can't- I can't- I just-

— For god's sake...

— It's not- It doesn't- It isn't- Yes yes here. I-

— One thousand. Count out one thousand.

The pasty slag opens the book. It's got bills in it held on with a paper clip. She counts out a grand an' still has a wad left over. I can see Nood's provoked. He stands up about to go over but I move first takin' the grand off them an' dumpin' the gear on the piano. I feel this big urge to leave. Nood don't budge. He looks the pair of them over.

— Have a nice rave an' don't do nothin' stupid cos the pigsa got dogs.

Nood looks at me like he's missed somethin'.

— An' the dogsa got noses that can sniff charlie for weeks after. Bein' legal bods you know the score innit.

We move to go. But Gillian's been watchin' too much news. She's a bit of a *have a go hero* an' starts yellin' livid tryina grab at Nood with her head shakin' all over.

— You have to pick on people don't you, she's screamin' or words to tha' effect.

Nood's just doggy paddlin' in her face to keep her off. After a bit she gives up. Stands there steamin'.

— Fulfilling is it? Enjoy your work do you? says Gillian close to tears.

— Every day's a challenge, says Nood real quiet. I was gonna be a paramedic bu' i' just wasn't stimulatin' enough. Na mean Gillian...

We turn out the lounge headed for the front door.

— You're *bloody*- You're a *bloody*... legume, shouts Gillian.

Nood stops in his tracks. So I have to pull him all the way out the door down the stairs an' back in the car.

— What's a... *legoom*? he says.

— Fuck do I know, I say strugglin' with the ignition.

Ten after three

I'm smart enough to drive til we're well down Swain's Lane an' out of the trees without so much as openin' my mouth to breathe. Back at the parade at the bottom of the Lane there's a delivery van blockin' the way so I'm gettin' very edgy glancin' in the mirror an' all over. A sweaty bastard an' his sidekick weighed down by a massive keychain are unloadin' bread rolls. Like one at a time.

— Won't be a mo', shouts Keychain cheerful.

We're in front of this café full of starchy assholes. Tables on the pavement an' people talkin' in low voices or posin' in movie star shades an' readin' big papers. There's a kid runnin' in circles with a balloon on a string. A car comes up behind so's I can't reverse out. Even with the window down there's no air. At every crossin' corner signpost there's always som'in ready to fuck me up. An' Nood's just sittin' there smug with himself an' his bigtimin'.

— Don' i' bother you man? This is the getaway.

— Si' tigh' be alrigh' on the nigh'. Na mean. Wicked, says Nood sniggerin'.

I'm tappin' on the wheel to get things movin' but the more I tap the less they move. Now Keychain's stopped a mo' to chat about the weather with some fuckin' postman. The kid with the balloon's joined by other kids with *their* balloons. Mums're gettin' to know each other. They're exchangin' favourite nappy stories. An' makin' jolly arrangements for the jolly weekend. An' Sweaty Bastard's bread rolls keep comin' out the back o' the van like jesus was organisin' it personal. I mean trees're swayin' there's laughter hangin' on the breeze an' the sun is just shinin' away in happy town.

I open the door an' get out. I'm takin' deep breaths to keep my heart goin'. I light up a cigarette.

— Tax... Wha' y'doin' Tax? says Nood gettin' out. Whass goin' on? Get in man he's abou' to move.

But I slam the door shut instead.

— Nood... Know wha'? I just figured out who you are? Yeah...

— How d'you mean? Wha' you–

— Yeah really I just figured it all out...

I lean over the top of the car an' shout:

— *Idyat bwai*. Innit. IDYAT BWAAAAI.

Nood's head's suddenly goin' three sixty with paranoia an' there's people in the café more or less cuttin' holes in their papers for the view.

— What?... Whassis? he's tryina whisper.

— In other words a *cunt*.

— Whassis in aid of?

— You know wha' the fuck it's in aid of.

Nood comes round to my side of the car lookin' round casual the whole time an' puttin' on a real showtime smile. He puts an arm over my shoulders.

— Tax what y'worried abou' we got a grand for a loada Marcello's table salt. Give 'em jokers a sting up the nose innit.

— Thass sweet only for one thing: Kingsley's gonna HACK OUR FUCKIN' HEADS OFF. YOU SHOULDA FUCKIN' TOLD ME.

— No need to steam y'fuckin' head off in front of café spaghole is there, says Nood tryina hide his mug.

But I'm comin' down off of all the gear an' I don't give a fuck. I push him in the chest.

— Shoulda fuckin' told me man I'm tellln' ya.

— Told you wha'? he says pushin' me back.

— You're a cunt. You shoulda fuckin' said.

— Wha' was I gonna-

— SHOULDA FUCKIN' SAID. Shoulda fuckin' said.

I wipe spit off my mouth.

— Listen man I was gonna-

I grab a fistful of t-shirt an' lean in so's our faces would fit onto a passport photo.

— Shoulda fuckin' told me y'sly piece o' cak- *Buddies*? Cunt. Wha'm I doin' goin' to y'fuckin' weddin'?

— Whassi' matter if I never told ya. Kingsley ain't gonna twig. He ain't never gonna know *nish*. Get off me ya-

— The fuck he ain't, I say pushin' him away.

He stumbles back but grabs onto me hard as he can with both hands clawed pullin' us both over the bonnet. We roll together on to the ground in a heap. Mainly to avoid really layin' in to each other. For a second we're tryina get grip on the gravel scrabblin' hard like we're fightin'. Then we're on our feet in some jumbled wrestlin' lock just facin' off sweatin'. Nood's gone red like he's healthy.

— NO HE AIN'T NO, he's yellin', NO. NO. He ain't gonna know *diddly doo*. Get off... Get y'fuckin' hands... So whassa fuckin' problem? Get offa me Tax. You got a chip on y'shoulder about i'?

— Nah the whole king edward. You're a cunt an' you know it. Y'shoulda fuckin' said. Kings-

— Kingsley ain't gonna know shit nish bollocks... An' I'll tell you why...

I just have to laugh at this even though what comes out my mouth is vergin' on hysterical. Nood lets go raisin' his hands like it's all over. So I backfist him in the chest an' let go. Nood grunts but don't protest. Just straightens his clothes.

— Kingsley-

— Ain't the fuckin' point Nood.

— Course it is.

— You stitched me up.

— Ain't the fuckin' point.

— Course it is.

I let loose a good kick at the car to add to the mornin's dents. Nood raises his arms an' lets them slap down on his thighs.

— D'y'wanna fuckin' know why or dontcha?

— Why wha'...? I say in half a mumble my whole soul groanin' in advance of the cak I'm gonna hear.

I feel sorry for Stell havin' to hitch up with the king of screwheads. Nood arranges his balls an' bends his head toward my ear with a *wait til you hear this* look on his face. Then starts talkin' to me like my brains got left in maternity.

— *Kings*-ley righ'...

I wanna punch his lights out an' grind my knuckle right in the side of his head.

— He'd have to *phone the bods up* righ' to *arrange* it yeah... a *deal* yeah-

— So fuckin' wha'?

— No lissen lissen: think it through... He'd have to *phone 'em up* righ' for a *deal* yeah an' they're not exactly gonna ask him round again in a hurry innit. For a *dinner* do. Or a *tea* party. Na mean. Not now they've *met* him. Least not til they find out where he sticks his fag ends...

Nood laughs pattin' my back and takes a big look round at the café.

— ...See wha'm sayin'. But the same time they're not gonna fuck him up either. Iss not like they ain't got manners na mean. Na mean. Kingsley calls they'll just tell him *no ta not today mister Kingsi sir.* So *Kings*-ley righ' he'll just *ashoom* they changed their minds. See? It's so simple it's brilliant yeah. Na mean... Marcello really come through on this one man...

Nood raises his arms smilin' an' full o' the joy o' life.

— So am I a cunt? Or am I an *idyat bwai*?

Tough choice. I got no steam left so we shake an' have a laugh. Wha' else am I gonna do.

— I don't care wha' people say Nood. To me you don't stink like a tub of pig shit.

— Hey? Eh? Oi. Who says...

I start goin' back in the car laughin'.

— Oi. Tax. Oi...

A coupla these crusty types in the café must think it's street theatre cos they're givin' us a round of applause. Nood soaks it up takes a bow an' is practically ready to give out autographs. Even pats a floatin' balloon back with a *there you go son*. The cunt.

Twenty five to four

The lane's cleared up. Guess the bread rolls must've run out which is a fuckin' miracle. The resident lush is passin' his hat round on Nood's behalf. We coast back into Kentish Town behind a convoy of boozy buses spewin' black. Nood's late for signin' an' the traffic's already buildin' up with cars queuin' in ratruns to turn onto the high street. Like how come these fuckers ain't at work? I stick the tape on to avoid talkin' but I hate the fuckin' music. It's Nood's music. Reminds me of Koom an' Riz an' the whole fuckin' thing. Nood gets straigh' off on it. He'd get off on an electric click track. He's right back into tappin' on the dash like someone put his batteries back in.

Cross the pissy canal over the junction an' down Jamestown. Sift through along the back of the high street to avoid the full-time tourists. Past a coupla pissy bars an' then a coupla pissy alleys. Finally park up round the pissy corner from the pissy dole office.

— Righ' where's me buzz ticket? says Nood steppin' out hands in pockets.

— Try the floor...

— Yeah righ', he says pickin' up his mashed dole card from the greasy backseat floor where it's been all week.

He shakes his *double R* bomber jacket off an' dumps it on the front seat. There's a dead metal clang as a jack hits the handbrake. He whips out a kuf wrap sticks in his thumb an' gives his gums a good rubbin'. Then with the kuf numbin' his face into a demon smile he pats an' shifts his hair with both hands into a whole new shape. He'd go far doin' dandruff ads. I glance round for Lendon.

— Jiffy, says Nood hitchin' up his jeans.

When he's done hitchin' he goes off to sign kinda adoptin' this pimp walk like he was wearin' a white suit an' cuban boots. There's chicks goin' in behind him who probably got done up just to sign on. Like the big moment of the day when there's people queuin' an' everyone's lookin' at whoever's signin'. Ten seconds of blindin' stardom. You go'a look street tuff an' act like you ain't takin' it from nobody. So when the sorry fuck behind the desk asks you to stick y'name down you look at them like they'd just shagged your mum an' told you she was crap. Suddenly the car gets a shove from behind.

In the rearview there's a white beemer with tinted windows. Lendon's already amblin' over glintin' in the sun an' arrangin' his leather baseball cap. I lean out the window an' he squats down bouncin' like he's springloaded. We shake.

— *Raggaganstamuthafucka.*

— How y'doin man, says Lendon laughin'.

— Shi'. I go' a weddin' to go to.

— Surprise me. Five innit.

— Yeah man. Bring y'sister.

— She'll be there she'll be there. I just go'a sort my jam roll. Nood signin'?

— He's learnin'.

— Yeah righ'. Free handwritin' lesson. Lord knows he needs it.

— You should know too. You went school with him...

Lendon's smile goes. He shakes his head. An' I know there an' then what he wants to talk about.

— Half the world wenna school with Nood Tax. Most of 'em's doin' slow death. The other half man: that's where you wanna be. Keep tellin' ya I know *people*.

— Wha' like Coca Cola *the world's a daisy chain* sor'a people?

Lendon pushes his cap back.

— Who you talkin' at man? This is me. Lendon.

— Sorry. Slipped my mind.

— Fuck... Tellin' you you should blow Nood out after he gets hitched. He ain't gonn' be good for *nothin'* anyhow. Stell'll be pumpin' out another Nood every year. *Twofold threefold* pressure. We should network na'm sayin'. You wanna hook up with the action. Guy's a fuckin' loser. I'm fifteen hundred a week serious. Yeah thass righ' man fifteen big. Guys I know the A to Z's their bible. Like they're sittin' round sayin' *pages forty through fifty's mine-*

— With lyrics like tha' you should be in the top ten na mean.

— So whass *your* big idea? I'm tryina do you favours an' you're dissin me man.

— Ain't dissin you no way. No way. Thing is I ain't about to-

— Why not man? Whass he doin' for you? Whass your end? I mean look at the state of these wheels.

— You stop to mash my bumper an' tell me that? I'm rushin' out to get a four wheeler.

— *Wise up lissen to the word in the muthafuckin' hood...*, says Lendon quotin' Rappa Freeze Dry or who.

— Yeah I'm listenin'. I mean look at yours man. If that car don't spell Dee Dee-

— Thass the point Tax. They look at the car an' think no way's mista gangstamuthafucka gonna drive it. An' they know that we know they know. So I drive it. One step ahead. Corn on the fuckin' cob double bluff.

— Yeah an' they'll catch y'with a triple.

— Wha'm I gonna tell you? says Lend shruggin'. Offer's open man. Make your move before it's too late. Thass why I'm here. I need my frontrunner y'na mean. Plenny of room where I'm standin'... For now...

He bounces up slappin' the roof.

— 'Preciate it man. Really. I'll let you know...

— Sooner the better na mean, he calls over his shoulder.

— Yeah an' bring Charmaine.

— Seen...

Lendon goes off burnin' rubber as he reverses down the sidestreet. He's got a point. I don't wanna wait all my life to get busted like those dickhead cabs parked up right outside the rock an' roll on the high street. Blinkers on an' aerials blowin' in the breeze. An' then they wonder why they get done by the social for fraud. Anyway.

We're fucked for time now with washin' an' dressin' an' shit an' Stell's mum still to pick up. I'm startin' to feel sick. Like *sick*. My eyes feel sore red. The traffic an' people an' noise. An' Nood's weddin' ain't even underway. I rest my head on the steerin' wheel. The plastic's hot an' sticky from sun an' too many corners curves bends. There's a piece of face reflectin' in the speedo. A nose with a number. Half a dark eye. Skin shinin' sweat. Bony an' busted. Someone like me. Far beyond sleep. Further'n any miles you could count. Beyond everythin' an' everyone. An' silent for a whole second. Just smellin' o' jasmine. Then Nood comes back gets in slammin' the door so's the car rocks.

— Cunts told me I go'a join the club.

I get back uprigh' in the seat.

— So wha' d'you say?

— I told 'em I was already in the club. *Wha' club's that then they say*... An' I go:

Nood creases an' grabs my arm.

— The HOOman fuckin' club. Wicked. Tellin' ya man I folded all over. But they just like... couldn't see it. Couldn't see the HOOmour na mean.

— Know the feelin'.

I have to listen to Nood singin' *country roads take me home* all the way up the backstreets to his yard. I stop off among kebab wraps an' shite leather jackets stalls an' broken up vegetable crates an' people floggin' second-hand levis to buy third-hand at first-hand prices. Assholes everywhere at all hours gobblin' fuckin' everythin'. Consumin' an' shittin' an consumin'.

— Sort you out in a bit Tax na mean, he says steppin' out. Cut up with Marcello later...

Course I don't like this arrangement cos you just don't fuckin' know but I can't say nothin'. Too wasted anyway.

— Safe. I know where to find ya.

— Yeah very funny. Ain't got too much on the clock so get back down ASA double P.

Nood sticks a king size blue of charlie in my palm.

— Point two five in there.

Guess it'll see me through a while. Then he opens up a bigger wrap that's full of selected charlie rocks.

— Special driver dab.

So I dab my finger onto a fat white yellow rock an' press it on my gums til it's gone. Nood groans out the car. I pull the door shut after him.

— La'er scumpig. Don't forget behind your ears.

— Yeah an' give Scheinbaum one for me, says Nood.

Ten to four

So I'm headin' to my place for the first time in fuck knows. Up Chalk Farm past the Roundhouse. Adelaide to Swiss Cottage where the lights're out an' it's mayhem with leery van drivers everywhere. One of 'em cuts me up so I give him some horn an' stick a finger at him. He stops the van in the middle of the road an' gets out like a fuckin' psycho. So I open my door an' show him a monkey wrench that I got stashed under the seat. It's enough to stop the fool dead. I drive past stickin' my finger out again.

Belsize down to West End Lane past the tube left onto Iverson an' right onto Maygrove to the Kilburn High end. I driven this so many times I just wake up when I'm there. I'm kinda relieved I don't have to take my split off of Nood there an' then. Wouldna felt right. But what woulda? We're stiffin' people left an' right an' I'm stiffin' him an' out there I just know there's people about to stiff us. Could be anyone. Probably someone we know. Park up near the viaduct that sits on the junction like a lid. A train crosses over.

I can already feel Mrs. Scheinbaum lookin' out the fuckin' window from behind the lace. Before I actually see her. I'm gettin' my keys ready but she's already openin' the front door. She just stands there with her tiny lipstick mouth all pursed up an' moist from where she licks it all the time like a fuckin' lizard.

— That's three weeks you owe... Oh yes... Oh yes... Don't think I don't know you've been sneaking out. Because I do.

I look her in the eye an' reach down my trousers. I take out the wad of money lookin' her in the face the whole time. Ain't even counted it yet an' it's a bit worse for wear after all day down there. I count out the rent plus a week advance an' give it over. Her mouth opens up a little bit like she's waitin' for a boiled sweet. She probably thinks I'm disgustin'. Can't tell in her eyes. Course she grabs the spondooli with both hands. She wants to say somethin' else but can't think what so I sor'a push past her an' go up. Half way up she remembers.

— Oh: about your car...

But a train goes over an' all I see is her gob movin' an' lips shinin' an' the light shakin'. In the room I throw my clothes off an' take out Koom's money. It's all in twennies. I count five fifty. That makes it close to six hundred with Riz's cut included. Koom an' Joey they ain't gonna let that rest. I leave the cash on the table by the window. The air's gone stale so I shove the window up far as it goes. Somewhere across the back lots there's this woman screamin' her minge off.

— WHY D'Y'DO I' TO ME YOU BASTARD. WHY D'Y'DO IT.

She's screamin' no matter what time. I shut the window again an' go through to the shower. I get in under it makin' sure the manky curtain doesn't touch my skin. Then I turn the tap. That first freezin' second wipes the day clean til the water starts steamin'. Face up I close my eyes.

I float down some river green yellow orange. I'm three sat in the bath with my sister. I'm on holiday in the sea. Dad's liftin' me for the view. Then I'm upside down. He had a lump of skin fillin' his belly button. Used to have nightmares about it. The lump fallin' out an' me bein' sucked in like down a plughole. I'm tryina hear what he's sayin'. But there ain't no voice in my dreams.

I open my eyes again when I remember Nood's weddin' an' star' to wash. Through a gap in the shower curtain I can see my suit on the bed where I laid it out days ago. Just to air it. Was gonna get it dry cleaned. Too black for a weddin' anyway. Too fuckin' bad. Three years the last time I wore it. More. There're still grass blades stuck to the shoes from Kensal Green cemetery. There was a drizzle. Not many people turned up. Them that did none of us knew. After it was over me an' mum an' Cee walked over the wet grass an' sat by a tree. Mum smoked a fag. An' I watched an ant crawlin' up Cee's leg.

I wash til I ain't been cleaner. Then I do the charlie an' get dressed with a fag in my mouth. Koom's money *my money* I put into a little bag. Wrap it tight an' balls it. Why I don't know. Should stash it here but it feels better with me. There's a sixteenth of personal which is a piece of leb I been savin' that I pocket for later.

I open the window again. She's still screamin' *you bastard why did you do it*... Cos he really loves you I'm thinkin'. I leave the window open. She might as well scream while I'm out. I check the room for signs. All I see's damp patches an' rotted frames an' gear you could pack in a carrier. I ain't been here. Then I comb up slip on a tie an' I'm out on the street again. I rev up the car just to give Scheinfuck migraine. It's what dad used to do to the whole street every fuckin' mornin'.

As I turn out the street Nood's tape ejects an' the radio kicks in distortin' between two channels. I'm reachin' out to flick the coathanger aerial into position. The sound kinda settles first on easy listenin':

Green P an' his Flute Boys play jazz greats for the high season...

A street away it jumps over to the news:

An elephant went on the rampage through Hampstead Heath today after escaping from a travelling circus and leaving its trainer dead. Police marksmen cornered the animal but were forced to shoot it near Hampstead High Street when it threatened passers-by. A police spokesman said: we had to put the safety of the public first.

I kill it open the window an' take a good lungful of stench. I try to think what it must be like to be an elephant.

Half four by now

Up Belsize Swiss Cottage Primrose Hill past the bridge an' down Gloucester. I get back to Camden with my head full. Koom Kingsley Kensal Green Scheinfuck. Nood. Rubbish blown into my head by accident. Stuff I wouldn't choose no more. People I'd like to fuck over then forget.

Clampers're workin' Nood's street like villains. They're pluckin' up big ones an' securin' 'em down to the flatbed like prizes. They wear gloves for the job only choosin' the ones that's just gonna pay an' go. Those that can pay now an' forever. An' they all got *whistle while you work* faces like they got a licence to scam an' ain't afraid o' nobody.

Nood's already out on the pavement lookin' like son of Kray an' tryin' not to scuzz his shoes in the filth. He's two-toned double-breasted with flappin' vents silver tie an' a white hankie pokin' out his top pocket. For the first time in his life he ain't treadin' in anythin'. I swing open the passenger door an' crawl up to him well impressed with the act.

— Lookin' spruce Nood...

Nood tiptoes in real careful like the car was dirty. Makes sure his suit's clear of the door an' closes it. He grins big.

— Feelin' spruce...

— Jesus man you're reekin' like a whore's handbag. Wha' the fuck is i'?

— Iss extra aroma na mean.

— Gi's some then.

— It's alrigh' innit, says Nood takin' an aerosol out his pocket. It's called *pot pourri*. Stell had another one called *pine forest* but-

— Nah...

So by the time we're only half way to Harlesden for Stell's mum the car's ripe. I have to double back across the bottom of Kilburn where I don't wanna be seen in a suit. Then the back of Kensal Rise through its narrow tight streets. On Palermo a bag lady with no mouth throws her bag at the car. Then drop in to Harlesden where every piece o' trash is a relic an' the sun don't shine 'less you pay subscription. There's so many heads a square foot you have to watch the lights the whole time in case some fuckin' asshole with a spliff hangin' out his mouth crosses them at two mile an hour when they're red.

Stell's mum's is in a quiet street near Willesden Junction. Nood directs me to stop up an' we do a couple more dabs of gak from Nood's bag. I stash the rest under the back seat. Nood looks at me sneerin' across his face like he was marlon brandhead.

— We're puttin' the squeeze on after all the ceremonies an' shit is over. You know that yeah. So don't go ge'in' loaded.

He pouts his mouth out an' straightens his tie like some slickdick salesman.

— Look alrigh' yeah.

I brush some imaginary shit off his jacket.

— Yeah man. You're the dog's bollocks.

He gets out the car looks at Stell's mum's gaff like it's his an' goes toward the door. Only the moment he starts walkin' he's arrangin' his dick. Reachin' right down his trousers an' sortin' himself out like Stell's mum wasn't doin' a Scheinbaum an' lookin' out some dark window for her future son-in-law. The front door opens then closes behind him like the hammer house of horror. I feel the charlie lockin' up the back of my throat. Then I hear this *boshin'* noise. Well regular. Well close. I'm gettin' sweated up just tryina figure what it is.

Through a thin gap between cars cross the road I see this even thinner kid with a yellow plastic crash helmet on. Ain't even five but you can tell it's *his* wall. His personal slice of pavement. Ain't even five an' he's givin' himself pressure. He's hittin' himself over the head with a piece of brick like he's testin' one or the other. *Bosh an' Bosh an' Bosh.* Could set a clock. There's a look in his eyes like he ain't poncin' about. Like he's practised this before. Like he'll go as far as he goes. Til he's good an' done. Til somethin' definite happens.

Minute later Nood's out with a coupla right takeaways. Both of 'em wearin' hats like pizzas. Probably Stell's grandma. The car doors open an' they get a whiff of the pot pourri.

— Oh smells lovely an' fresh in 'ere, says Stell's mum.

Nood gives me a thumbs up.

— Special weddin' service Mrs. Stell, I say.

— Oh is it now. A nice thought from the best man eh. Call me Marion an' this is me mum Elly. In y'get.

— Stings me chops.

— What does mum?

— That rotten whiff. Got it in me mouth.

The two of them finish pilin' in the back an' Nood shuts the door after them real polite. Then he comes round the front gets in an' clears his suit all round. Shuts the door. Locks it. Then he fishes round for what used to be the seatbelt. Connects it up. Jams his tape back in.

— Floor i' Tax.

DOG DOG TSSS DOGGA DOGGA DOG TSSS

Ten to five

So I'm floorin' it down Harrow Road past the junk holes cab joints an' fast foods. Past skankers angled over railings drawin' on cider an' beer. Past the Scrubs Lane junction an' along the cool dark wall of Kensal Green cemetery. But we ain't takin' the corners too good with the extra load. They're just gettin' all jumbled up in the back with Elly holdin' her hat on like her head come with it.

To me it's clear whatever time we get there it ain't gonna be the right time however fast we're goin'. Make the lights at Ladbroke Grove then the junction of the Great Western. By now Nood's leanin' well forward strainin' on the belt. He's tappin' an' slappin' the dash like he's zappin' aliens in a computer game. Judgin' by the vein bustin' out his temple an' the little bleepin' sounds comin' out his mouth he most likely is.

— Can't you slow it down a bit. Only mum's turnin' green an' that music I mean is it appropriate?

— Wha'? Sorry Mrs Marion. Nood? *Nood.*

— Wha'... Eh? Whassa' Marion?

— Slow it down a bit. I don't want to have to send Stell off from an ambulance. An' the music...

— Sorry Marion. Sorry gra'ma you alrigh'? Sorry yeah? Sorry Tax take it easy an' turn i' down, says Nood returnin' from Moonbase Ten.

He looks round every which way to get his earth bearings then swings round toward the back seat again.

— Lookin' forward to the do then gra'ma?

Elly keeps stumm ignorin' him an' smilin' out the window like people was cheerin' her down the street. She don't like Nood on account of Nood's mum Carole dissin Stell or som'in. But that ain't stoppin' Nood.

— Like a bit of a rave up does she Marion?

— She'll 'ave a couple alright. Won't you mum?

— Did you remember to bring me dried fruit?

— You know I did mum...

Marion smirks at me in the mirror.

— ...I've got the pineapple chunks in me bag an' I already gave you the papaya squares so-.

— What about-?

— Don't even ask about the prunes. You forgotten wha' happens when you get onto those? says Marion grinnin' at me in the mirror. I left 'em home for your own good alrigh'?

But the old prunehead don't like it an' likes it even less when Nood's grinnin' in her face.

— Hey Marion. Whassa legoom?

— A legoom? A *legume* don't you mean? Rings a bell. What d'you wanna know that for?

— Somebody called him one, I say.

Elly starts chucklin' away to herself with her hand coverin' up her chops. Nood smiles.

— I think she knows som'in we don't know innit Marion.

— Go on 'en mum what's a legume?

I see in the mirror she uncovers her mouth for a split second of yellow denture.

— Type o' vegetable, she whines.

We all piss ourselves except Nood who sinks in his seat.

— Cane it, he tells me out the corner of his mouth.

But as we go under the flyover cuttin' through the amber light an' onto Marylebone I notice the cops. How long their van's been sittin' out there alongside I don't know but they're signallin' us to pull over. They're some kinda crowd control unit in a van that's got all the showroom options like steel mesh over the windows an' a bumper like a bulldozer. No sunroof.

— Shouldna gone so fast. I better do the talkin'.

— No worries Marion. I'll sort 'em, says Nood playin' flashcash son-in-law ready to bung the whole fuckin' vanload a fiver.

Nothin' for it. So just past Lisson Grove I signal my intention to pull over an' bring the vehicle to a controlled standstill accordin' to the spirit of the highway code.

— They'll put the lot of us away this time, says Elly.

— An' bring back hangin' for you gra'ma, says Nood.

I get out the car tellin' Nood to stay put but he gets out as well with Marion behind him. Three mouths is three times the truth. Couldn't be worse. The cops're already out the van an' separate me an' Nood an' leave Marion hoverin' about. I s'pose they surround the car in case Elly makes a run for it. One of 'em leans in the window an' starts chattin' away.

The spotty cop nearest me looks in my direction. He's focusin' on the brim of his hat so's he looks cross-eyed or stupid. An' his mouth is open like a fish. His chief prods him in the back. I suddenly realise they're all cartoon rookies on their first day out. Pimple takes a breath an' launches righ' in.

— Going anywhere in particular sir?

— Well yeah as it goes.

— We're really late for my daughter's wedding officer. It's supposed to be at five down the Euston-

— This your car is it?

— Yeah thass righ'.

— They're just driving us. That's my son-in-

— Ladies with you are they?

— Yeah thass righ'.

— It's my daught-

— Going to a wedding you say?

— Yeah thassi'.

— My daughter's g-

— Carrying any tools at all are you?

— Thass- No. Wha' sor'a tools? Ain't carryin' no tools-

— Asking about the tools Sarg...

Nood's out of earshot but I can tell he's wired. Fidgetin' round. Buttonin' unbuttonin' his jacket. Lookin' at the boot like he's seein' the porn mags draped all over it an' he's all set to break down an' confess. The cop's even handin' him some papers an' documents an' fuck knows. Meantime Marion's linked arms with me like she's workin' some secret psychology on 'em. Only nobody else gives a shit. Policeboy Pimple's still on the case thinkin' through his whole hard soft approach.

— Well go on then, says Sarg.

Pimple clears his throat. He's playin' for time which ain't exactly doin' us favours.

— Know about *the march* do you? says Pimple to the clouds.

I'm abou' to answer but he raises a hand turnin' to Sarg but not sayin' nothin'. So Sargie give him his best uncle smile to get some kinda action.

— Is it alright calling it *the march* Sarg?

— Well, says Sarg real mellow, is it about a lot of people walking together in a rhythmical manner down a prearranged route?

— To the best of my knowledge yes Sarg it is.

— So what do you think? Sarg asks him flashin' me a quick smile.

Pimple's lost for words. I mean he's lost full stop. Truth is he's one fucked up confused hooman who ain't gonna make it through probation. So I cut in.

— Nah mate. I don't know abou' no march. Wha' march?

— Says he doesn't know about *the march* Sarg. What shall I do now? Look in the car? Look in the boot? Take a butchers at the tyres? Tax disc? Run 'em all through the PNC? Call-

But it's clear Sarg ain't really up to listenin' to no more fool questions or even thinkin' them up.

— Nah. Daughter's wedding is it madam?

— Yes that's right. Old Town Hall Euston R-

— We'll escort you down madam. Just follow on.

Off he goes. I track him step at a time back to his van waitin' for the catch. Pimple sor'a fiddles with his belt like it was holdin' in his self-respect. Then he ain't got no choice but to poodle after Sargie. The rest of 'em're sayin' their goodbyes to Elly an' Nood an' Marion an' movin' toward the van. *Nice of you to come* I'm thinkin'. I'm lookin' at Nood to shed any kinda light on the situation. He sidles up wide-eye an' shrugs so's his neck almost disappears between his shoulder blades.

— Asked my one for details o' my local neighbourhood watch scheme. He said they needed people like me.

I nod like it's all just fallen into place. They signal us to get started. So we all pile back in. *They* all pile back in. They stick their lights on. I stick mine on. The traffic ease up to make space for the circus van an' we sift onto the Euston Road behind it like real important specialties. I'm even smilin' at the cops all sardined in the back. Marion's blowin' big pouty kisses. I could bust out in tears of joy. Nood's gone sweaty an' emotional like he's discovered religion. Only Elly looks disappointed. She's rackin' her brains figurin' what they missed.

— Couldn't they find nothing then?

Nood just cracks up.

— Didn' even get a producer gra'ma... Wha' d'y'think o' tha'? Eh? Send off or wha' Marion.

— It's a righ' send off if we get there bu-

— We'll fuckin' get there now, says Nood clenchin' a fist. Fuckin' escor'. Fuckin' wicked. Pardon the french bu' they're gonna love this innit Tax. *Love* it. Wait til they hear this na mean. 'Kin' 'ell. WI-KED na mean Tax.

— Yeah man wicked...

But in all this cartoonin' somethin' still don't feel tickety boo.

— So whassi' all about then Marion this march?

— Got the Nazis marchin' down Hyde Park. Was in the papers.

— Yeah? So we're s'posed to be Nazis innit Tax.

— Yeah righ'. Four tooled up Nazis on our way to a weddin'. Thass why we get the escort.

— Wicked...

Nood sticks the ring in my breast pocket pats it an' settles down for the home run through the rush hour. He's well pleased with life. In the back they fret about Stell the time the registrar the prunes an' the sausages. Out in front a burst of sun trips me out an' turns the windscreen into this scratched up haze coverin' the whole fuckin' town. For a second I can't see shit 'cept a flashin' blue strobe. An' wha'm I doin'? Followin' it...

The sun fades an' the scratches become the turrets of Saint Pancras stickin' out everywhere an' black from fumes like the church of doom. Then I glance across the road through cones an' people an' layers of vans an' trucks an' diesel risin' through the warm air.

They're all there. Standin' dead still lookin' out in a group in front of the town hall with everythin' movin' on the Euston Road 'cept them. The guys. Lendon an' his sister Charmaine an' his auntie Noreena in her day out gear. Ez Deezee Zeb with their backin' singers Jace an' Daisy. Stell in white. Stell's sister Mannie with her hoodlum kid. Nood's mum Carole. Kings an' Baba an' the video man an' Shitsky Shuddupsky an' a sax an' a whole buncha guys an' a whole buncha Stell's broads. An' if ever they all could see with one eye the same thing then it's right now as we do the drive-by with Sarg an' PC Pimple spreadin' the traffic like Moses an' his crew with blue lights on.

Well late

I give it some horn an' they all come back with wavin' an' shoutin'. Mainly in distress on seein' all them *Poh-lice*. Lendon's coverin' up his *known but not wanted* mug with a hand. Baba's movin' Kingsley as far away from Nood an' the car as possible. An' the rest o' the crowd's fifty per cent thinned out like Mister Magic just tapped his top hat.

The cops do a U-ey in the middle of King's Cross an' I follow 'em round to the town hall. A coupla uniformed hands wave us an' I flash 'em back. Stell's rushin' up to the car dress all frothy white shoutin' above the noise of trucks an' shit.

— NOOOOD. FUCKIN' 'ELL. Shift y'cock the Geezer's doin' his nut in there.

— Babes babes—

— *MY GOD* wha' on earth took you so long? Carole's screamin' as we're scramblin' out.

— High pressure over Scandinavia wa'ni' mum. But did y'see that? Did- GUYS. Did- The fuckin'- The FUCKIN' PIGS GI'S AN ESCORT.

Stell an' Carole get drowned out with cheerin' an' shouts of *wicked* an' *Noo Dell*. Lendon says he'll take care of the car an' we move in a crowd toward the doors with Stell up front.

— Be'er have some bread on you Nood cos we ain't got fuck all to pay the registration fee. Didn't think of tha' did ya.

— We'll have a whip round.

— I don't believe it Stevie.

— Mum not now-

— But Stevie-

— An' don' fuckin' call me Stevie.

The video man's gettin' all this down for the nine o'clock news an' the mums're already mixin' it tryin' to be the first through the doors with a *he's my son she's my daughter* double act. Inside the swing door Nood gets a whip round goin' an' Kings an' Baba get burned for the whole fee cos of course they wanna look flush in front of everybody.

The Geezer's standin' well pissed off flappin' his papers round tryina get the show sorted. He gets the key personnel up front an' marches us to the room which might as well be a custody suite at Pimple's local nick. It's all striplight an' formica. Before they're even settled at the back he's straight into the whole routine. Some of the guys're still takin' calls.

— Yeah yeah safe be there in twenny, says Ez.

— Certainly that can be arranged sir, Kingsley hums into the mouthpiece.

— Wicked man. I was well tranced. Mee' ya down Brickhouse for the rinse na mean, says Deezee sharin' his life with the whole room.

— Will the gentlemen at the back please refrain from using their mobile telephones during the-

— Hey sorry priest. We're tot'ly refrained now. Innit Deez, says Ezra.

— He ain't no priest, says Deez.

The Geezer fixes his steamy little specs an' turns to Nood who's got his hands clasped together in front an' head bowed like he was before the head teachagangsta.

— Please repeat after me... I do solemnly declare...

— I do solemnly declare, says Nood.

Well after them words the place goes silent apart from Nood's mum who starts blubbin'.

— ...that I know not of any lawful impediment...

— ...tha' I know no' of any lawful... impemident...

This sets everyone off again with a round of laughter an' splutterin' an' Lendon shoutin' as he comes in late:

— Thass why you only got to be *deputy* homework monitor innit Nood?

Nood's abou' to step forward an' challenge this point so the Geezer raises his voice.

—...why I Steven Charles Lynch...

— Charles? goes Lendon.

— ...why I Steven... *Charles* Lynch...

— ...may not be joined in matrimony to Estelle Suzanna DaSilva.

— ...may no' be joined in matrimony to Estelle Suzanna DaSilva.

Shitsky takes her name as his cue an' starts in on his sax solo. He gets three notes out before Ez an' Deez manage to pull the fuckin' thing out his mouth.

— Don't wai' for the bird's bit will ya, says Ez.

— Mudder never could count in, says Shuddupsky laughin'.

— Hey: fokk you tokkin about?

Shitsky wipes his mouth with the back of his hand an' stands there swingin' his weight around with his head down like the music was still goin'. The Geezer's really had it by now an' is racin' Stell through her bit too fast for his own good.

— I do solemnly declare that I know not of any lawful impemi indep— iment why I Steven sorry *Estelle* Suzanna Silver *DaSilva* may not...

I wonder about all the times he's had to serve up this pudding. An' all the types of people who come in front of him an' whose names go through his head. An' out again.

An' all the times he's stood there like a livin' joke cos he ain't got his people with him. If he's got any. Cos that's how it should be: him standin' there with his crew takin' no bullshit from nobody.

— I call upon these persons here present...

Cos what is he without his people 'cept a guy in specs with a rash creepin' up his neck cos of all the shit goin' down.

— ...to witness that I Steven Charles Lynch...

Least if you got people there's always someone dumber'n you to laugh at an' shove around.

— ...do take thee...

But if you're on y'tod the whole time you're a sad cunt no two ways an' you deserve what you get an' can't fuckin' complain when you get it.

— Tax. Oi. *Tax*. TAX.

I realise Nood an' Stell an' everyone else is lookin' at me so now I'm the joke. Nood's reachin' toward me snappin' for the ring so course I do the pocket-slappin' gag mainly cos I can't remember where the fuck it is which makes the HOOmour a lot better for everyone.

— Nood's had to leave the ring for deposit on a big one Stell. But don't worry: iss comin' tonigh', Lendon's shoutin' to more laughter.

— Gaaaaaaaaaaaa.

— Gaaaaaaaaaaaa.

Through all the other laughs I hear these two comin' from the back that I know is from Koom an' li'l Joey. When they snuck in I don't know. I give over the ring. They ain't even s'posed to be here til the do so the hairs on the back of my neck're prickin' an' I don't wanna look round.

From behind I feel everyone's eyes on me. I glance over at Nood. He's smilin' straight ahead at the back wall of the room like it was his reflection. An' Stell's only got eyes for him. In the light there's a pale bit on her neck. A line between where the brown make-up stops an' her dress begins. Like a fillin' in a sponge cake. An' I'm lookin' at Elly an' she's got one too under her chin. An' Nood's got one too by the side of his nose where he couldn't see it if he looked. An' if he's got one then I'm thinkin' if there's a pale bit somewhere on me. Somewhere everyone can see. The back of my neck. On my ear. Somewhere I can't see. Somethin' that marks me out. An' they all fuckin' know. They fuckin' know. An' they're all playin' along with my whole fuckin' story like I was a cunt. They're all lookin' at me like I was a fuckin' cunt. But there's no way any of them's gonna put one over on me. I keep a step ahead of all of them. Only it's a real step. I know this is charlie talk. Asshole talk. *Flush all the gear down the hole when it's only y'mum at the door* talk. Nood talk. Like Nood has to triple bluff Mac everytime he goes out in case the fuckin' parrot's a canary. I dunno... I dunno... I get anxiety... I can't have a pale bit anywhere cos my skin's fuckin' grey all over all the time no matter what the fuckin' light. An' they probably all know.

— ...that I Estelle Suzanna DaSilva do take thee Steven Charles Lynch to be my lawful wedded husband...

— ...that I Estelle Suzanna DaSilva do take thee Steven Charles Lynch also know as Nood innit to be my bloody awful wedded husband...

Nood an' Stell take hold each other's hands. For a second I think they're in love. Somewhere after that both of 'em get declared husband an' wife a few times an' I sign my name as a witness. To wha' it ain't clear. But Stell's broads start hollerin' as Stell gives Nood's balls a quick feel on the Geezer's table. Shitsky busts loose with *here comes the bride* an' then it's all out of control. Auntie Noreena's chuckin' confetti left an' right before the Geezer can stop her. Mannie's kid gets airborne an' bombs the video man with a half-eaten mandarin yoghurt. Then the kid tries to get away from the scene of the crime so Mannie's gotta trap him on the floor with a chair.

I see Kingsley reachin' for the Geezer an' stickin' a tenner in his shirt pocket. Can't hear what they're sayin' only the Geezer's tryina push Kings away with both hands. When he takes out the bill an' tries to give it back Kings snatches it an' shoves it down his pocket even harder. So the Geezer takes it out an' so on.

'Ventually they get us to leave the place without bloodshed. We tumble out into the stinkin' road movin' into the sidestreet for the cars. I'm tryina avoid lookin' at Koom but his bandaged up nose makes it difficult. While Stell's sortin' out who goes in where Nood puts his arm round Koom like he's joshin' around.

— Alrigh' Koom? How's kebabs?

— Yeah man alrigh'. Nice do.

— Ain't begun na mean.

Nood starts walkin' Koom toward this phone box an' he blinks at me to follow.

— Jus' go'a make a quick one Koom.

— An' I got go wiv ya?

Nood opens the door of the phone box. Inside it's plastered in pink an' red an' yellow cards. Nood picks one out.

— Gi's ten pence.

Koom looks at me eyes twinklin' adjustin' his bandage but I look at my shoes. He pulls out a ten pee scratchin' the side of his number one cut where there's music notes shaved in.

— Gaaa. Wha' y'gonna do Nood? Whass Stell gonna say? Na mean.

Nood punches out the number on the card winkin' at Koom. I'm lookin' at Koom for signs that he knows who done him. It's weird but with his nose covered he ain't Koom no more. More like Robomoron. Can't tell what he's thinkin'. Nood searches the sky then looks in the refund flap just in case while he's waitin' for the answer. Koom's touchin' an' scratchin' his bandage kinda unsure of everythin'.

— Gaaa...

— Hello hello yeah za' the Australian blond? ....No no no lissen I don't give a monkey's abou' the measurements I jus' wanna know one thing yeah...

Nood looks at Koom who's tryina figure it all.

— How much for a fuckin' good hidin'?

With that Nood creases up so's I have to help him out the phone box. I sort of half shrug at Koom like to say *crazy fuckin' guy inn'e*. But Koom's already walkin' away shakin' his head. Nood's squeakin' with laughter.

— Tax Tax see his face?

— Mostly no as i' goes.

— Whass the joke? Wha' happened? Whass 'e laughin' abou'? says Stell comin' over all flushed in the face.

— Joy overcome him.

— An' we ain' even done the drugs yet innit Tax, says Stell.

Yeah right. So we pick Nood up an' carry him to the vehicle. Jace an' Daisy're stickin' white streamers to everyone's doors an' aerials an' there's this grunge metal pumpin' out of Ezra's van that's louder'n the rush hour itself. Twenny guys revvin' up ready to wade through the traffic like steamers. All fired up for the show.

Baba an' Kings've even sorted out a coupla Stell's broads for the back seat. An' who does Stell sort *me* out with? The fuckin' generation gap. Nood's mum. Auntie Noreena. Mannie an' the kid. Nood looks at me from the back of Lendon's an' makes out a cross on his chest. Then I see Lend's sister Charmaine comin' over. To help with the talk I guess.

Sometime after six

I get Charmaine to sit up front an' we merge into the traffic which ain't goin' nowhere. Mannie's kid starts in.

— Muuum: can I have a drink now mum?

— You've 'ad four cans o' fizz in two hours. Iss comin' out your ears.

— Bu' mum I nev- I nev- I never finished my drink.

— Robbie if y'don't shut i' now you'll- Take your hands off Auntie Noreena's dress... Sorry 'bou' that.

— Don' worry. I got a little bit o' chocolate in my bag. You gonna like that aren't you?

— Wha' d'you say to Auntie Noreena?

— Bleuuuggh.

So Nood's mum an' Auntie Noreena start fussin' over the kid in the back. I'm hopin' between the three of them they'll keep the sick little fuck under control. Char looks at me out the corner of her eye an' leans in.

— Nood fixed you up good boy, she says in this kinda low voice that creeps up my spine.

— Y'na mean. Figures today he can do what the fuck he wants. An' I'm hundred per cent here to help in any possible way you name it.

— Fair's fair.

— Yeah but there's weddings tha' last all the way to divorce. Ain't puttin' up with it til then.

— Whassa difference? You been puttin' up with it since time innit.

— A little while yeah.

— Like how long?

— A while is all...

I feel like Char's soundin' me out. Like I ain't seen her some time. She knows I had a thing for her. So now I'm the sensitive type who listens to her stuff which is mostly 'bout Lendon an' his *gangsta ways*. I just wanna get her off my case. 'Sides I ain't even in her league. There is that too.

— So how come you don't come round no more? You're only up the street... Busy righ'? Like wha' you been doin' 'part from scuzzin' round town with Nood?

— Oh I dunno. Scuzzin' round town with Nood far's I can remember. You?

— I go work. In the real world. You know? Last time I saw you you was talkin' big 'bout some new business. Your very own *littahl ting*.

— Oh that yeah... Was just an idea...

— So wha' happened?

— Well... I still like the freedom of the open road innit.

— Oh *pa-lease baby*. I hear all that from Lendon. He's bustin' with it.

— I'm jus-

— NO ROBBIE. I said no an' no means NO.

— MuuuuuUUUM.

— He's dropped som'ing on the floor Tax. Hope he don't mess up the car. He's like tha', says Mannie leanin' forward. I'll have to sor' ou' some entertainment when we get there. Keep 'im occupied...

— Like electric shock torture.

— Yeah, says Mannie laughin', I'll put 'im in the toilet an' throw the electric fire in. Innit.

— Yeah Mannie. Do wha' you go'a do.

Her an Auntie N are tryina prevent the kid takin' over the back seat but it's like he's got more legs than an octopus. I look at Char. She's smilin' to herself smoothin' down her hair but I catch her eye as we crawl along in first.

— Whass tha' look for? I wasn't ge'in at you before Tax.

— Yeah you were. An' you ain't even started. It's the same every time I see you. Pro'ly why I talk big innit.

— You ain't the only one trust me. You all talk big. Wheelin' dealin'. Duckin' divin'. Chargin' abou'. Iss like one of them spoof shows innit: *The GangstaGuys*.

She shifts in the seat. I can't help lookin' at her legs most of which I can see cos of these seventies style hot pants she's wearin'. I always think of her as warm. Warm legs. I'd like to do a long long line of toot all the way along her leg.

— You know Lendon-

— Lissen Char don' ask.

— I ain't said nothin' yet. Jesus guy...

— Well say i' then.

— Whass with you?

I take a breath. There's no air anywhere. In here. Out there. What was it he said dad. A rain'll come. Som'in' like that. It better. Only drizzled for him. I hate this fuckin' suit. Open my top button an' half lean out the window to get some traffic in my face. But Char won't let it go.

— Lendon jus'... I see where it's all gonna end up is all.

— Yeah? Who's talkin' *spoof stylee* now. Madame Charmaine looks in her crystal ball an' tells you where you're goin'. Kilburn in Lend's case.

— Nowhere in Lend's case.

— Well least he's still goin' nowhere. Some of them're fuckin' there.

— Serious man...

— Serious wha' Char? Whass the idea? Wha' d'y'want from me?

— ...Cos you an' him- I mean he's gonna listen to you na mean. Thing is we used to be close me an' Lend... Bu' these days I couldn't get a weather report na mean. He's-

— *Oh yeah sure*, I say tryina sound New York, *so I godda talk to da guy*. I'm gonna tell him look Lendon promise to change your pants an' I'll help you write your CV. Sorted.

— You're full of it... You know? I'm ask-

— Ask wha'?

Char takes a breath. I'm wonderin' which one of us is gonna live long enough to see the end of this.

— I'm askin' you this, she says measurin' out the words like rocks of premier kuf, cos he ain't lissenin' to no one.

— Well he ain't gonna listen to's sister is he? Nor me come to that. Me Char? Wha'm I gonna say me? Fuck...

— Leas' he's gonna-

— No he ain't. Lend's got all typesa ideas an' he ain't lissenin' in no direction. Wha' can I say? Thassi'.

— Thass exac'ly it. The whole o' Stonebridge is crawlin' with losers who ain't got yam between their ears. It's gangster Benidorm innit. Everyone goes for the cheap deals. So where's Lend? He's down with 'em too. Hangin' out with gangsters don't you know...

— *Hangin' out with gangsters*: you sound... I mean... Who ain't na mean.

She leans back an' looks out touchin' her hair to make sure there's no loose strands messin' her perfect sleek hairdo.

— You know thass shit. The whole bunch of 'em're *jokersmokers* na'm sayin'. All of 'em. Only Lend ain't even like that.

— I know: deep down he's an insurance salesman.

— You've always got some answer...

I wanna tell her not to go all mumsy but she's enough wound up already an' I know she'd really throw one.

— Wha'm sayin' is-

Char's cut by a snore from the back which is sick little fuck with no more fizz to keep him steamin'. Auntie N an' Carole're gigglin' between themself. Mannie's praisin' the almighty. Char just carries on but she's go'a be flaggin' by now.

— ...I'm sayin' all day every day he's talkin' *beemers an' bitches*. Thassi'. Beemers an' bitches beemers an' bitches beemers an' bitches. Y'na mean. Or the price of mobiles an' coke. An' bitches. Na'm sayin'. Thassi'. Thass his life.

— I'd settle for that.

— Nah you wouldn't.

— Fuck d'you know what I'd settle for? Lendon's tryina do his *littahl ting* is all. Just guys innit. Just guys is all.

— Guys... fuckbrains. Like they should set up some dance academy 'cept for *gangsta muthafuckas*. An' at the end instead of a show they should just do the drugs an' kill each other. Hook it up to cable. Order in the sixpacks. Make it a fam'ly affair.

— Yeah... well... You got a point: leas' dead none of 'em can sign on. And with *all the savings they make* they could open a new community centre.

Char touches her hair to make sure the style's still holdin' like she musta done a million times already an' like she's tired of the same fuckin' soap. But soaps never end. Just a bunch of people waitin' for the big one. An' talkin' big in the meantime.

The traffic's openin' up an' everyone's 'celeratin' down to Edgware Road. Ez comes alongside hangin' out the window passin' a spliff at forty miles an h. The three Shitskys are behind him tailgatin' right up his ass with Shitsky himself in the back blowin' on his horn. The rest of them are probably figurin' how to give some fat slag in a merc a good clean for her credit cards.

I been avoidin' lookin' in the mirror so's I don't have to talk. But I find myself eyeballin' Nood's mum so I'm predictin' she's go'a start. Char was bad enough. Nood's gonna get fuckin' shit for this. Carole makes a big deal of pushin' her face all the way into the front.

— We nearly there? she says warmin' up.

— Be there in a jiffy, I say without thinkin'.

— In a jiffy, says Carole laughin'. That's what Stevie's

always saying. In a jiffy this in a jiffy that but I don't know what he ends up doing with himself...

— Ha ha yeah Nood eh...

Char' s no fuckin' help. She just looks out the window pissed off. Which I guess is my fair due.

— It's funny but... you being called Taxi... you know you're Stevie's best man and I don't even know your proper name...

Carole laughs an' looks around but nobody 'cept me's listenin'. Auntie Noreena's feedin' sick little fuck in his sleep with a king size mars bar. Mannie's takin' a break an' dreamin'. Charmaine's pro'ly workin' on a permanent hump.

— So what is it then your real name? says Carole keepin' her laugh goin'.

— Ezekiel Mohammed Winston Charleybottom-Smythe an' I got three sixes on the back of my head.

— Oh blimey... S'pose I better stick with Taxi then.

— Easier innit.

I grin to let her know it's a joke. Keeps her quiet for a bit but I know she ain't done. By now the convoy's under the flyover an' filterin' onto the Harrow Road. We're all gettin' split up at the roundabou' an' I realise there's some kinda race on when Kings an' Baba burn past with Lendon in hot pursuit. Nood an' Stell snoggin' in the back. Nothin' I can do. Char looks at me sour.

— Charmaine-

— So d'you work with Stevie then? says Carole. He says you sometimes work together. Like partners.

— In crime Carole... Jus' kiddin'.

— So what is it you do then?

— More like who... Jus' kiddin'.

— Is he always like this?

Char's thinkin' up some smart answer to that but luckily can't.

— He don't have to be na mean.

— Well go on then what do you do?

I have to tell myself to take a deep breath. Feel like Pimple lost an' playin' for time. Searchin' for the righ' answers to the wrong questions.

— I had a job a while back bu' got the boot...

They're 'spectin' me to carry on but I'm hopin' for an embarrassin' silence. An' they're both hopin' the other one's gonna ask the questions. 'Ventually Carole can't hold her suspense no more.

— What was that then? The job...

— Oh some naff job. Ain't worth talkin' 'bou' really...

But everyone's waitin' all ears now. Start some dumb fuckin' story an' no matter how fuckin' dumb everyone'll sit there listenin' out for the next thing that happened even if nothin' ever could.

— ...Finsbury Park. I was in a basement factory type thing with a hundred people. All we's doin' all day was writin' *PARKER* with a special tool on some cheap joker pens na mean.

We drive another million miles an' we're still on Harrow Road. There's a trickle of sweat runnin' down my back. All the way to the crack. Sometime charlie makes me rage. Now I need a hit to keep the rage away. My story's got loose ends that Carole's jus' gaggin' to tie up. But I ain't gonna make it easy.

— Well... It's... a bit different I s'pose.

I glance a' Carole in the mirror. She knows she's got all the time she needs for this shit.

— Wha' from?

— Well... dunno...

Carole points at somethin' out the window. Then she looks round fans her face an' smiles first at Mannie's kid then Auntie Noreena. Then she checks the length of her arms like they'd grown since this mornin' or the sun had turned them blue. An' all of this is her act. Her big fuckin' act so's she can ask her big fuckin' question. I wait...

— So... why d'y'get the sack then? she asks like it just popped into her head.

— 'Spute with the chief.

— And...

— And nothin'. Big E.

Now I can feel Charmaine lookin'. Makes me feel like I ain't washed. An' the Harrow Road ain't gettin' shorter.

— Well go on: wha' d'y'do guy? Musta done somethin' na mean.

— It's not what *I* done...

— Well? goes Char.

— Well wha'... Truth be told... I slugged him in the mouth. Alrigh'?

— Oh blimey... You mean you hit him. The boss...

— Thassi' exactly in a nutshell Carole... He's grabbin' hold of some Somali woman. Na'm sayin'? In his office. No more'n five two an' she couldn't you know *spikka Eeenglish*. Straight off the fuckin' boat. So...

— You did that? You smacked him?

— Yeah Char yeah he was well out of order. She was as good as dumb. Couldn't say nothin'. She didn't have no power. Cos half of it's words innit. The way you rap. If y'ain't got that you need a machete na mean. Specially in a joint like that. Walk all over y'otherwise... Tell me I'm wrong.

Can see they're all well impressed. Which don't hurt. Truth be told I slugged him anyway. Only found out later about what he did to the slave labour. Amounts to the same thing though: a cunt with a busted lip. An' it amounts to nothin'. The lip's healed up an' the cunt's got a five stone refugee under him for one fifty an hour.

For the rest of the journey nobody says nothin'. They're all chilled out peaceful. Maybe the dull dronin' traffic an' heat's made them all drowsy silent. Quiet for a second. Not me.

Seven

Eventually our convoy bottlenecks round the Kilburn Lane lights people havin' tried an' tested a loada useless shortcuts. Lendon an' Baba're arguin' out their cars about who won some bet. We turn off through the red hootin' an' charged an' park up wherever we can around the beat up fucked up stinkin' Slice of Heaven. My clothes're stickin' my bladder's bustin' I can't breathe an' I'm gaggin' for charlie. Charmaine's comin' out of daydream tryina catch my eye like it's all ok really but I'm too fucked to look at her.

Once I'm out the car I just let the crowd flow around me. Let it carry me in. Let it go where it goes an' turn where it turns. Everyone's up an' runnin' linkin' arm slappin' back pointin' out. Laughin' at every joke goin' like they're bein' rationed. Baba bumps into me with a *hey sorry man* an' sparks my cigarette. Koom's doin' a take on Lendon's street bop an' Lend's pissin' himself. Nood's got his arms round Jace an' Daisy. Shitsky's wobblin' along serenadin' whoever. Ez an' Deezee an' them're makin' sure all the doors in front are open wide an' ready to receive. I'm in the middle. Flowin' with the whole thing. I'm a part of it like it was a part of me. I'm protected all sides by teeth noses hair eyes of people like a tide you just go'a roll with.

We head in to the back bar room where there's three long tables laid. White covers napkins in glasses full sets of cutlery an' daffs on every table. A bunch of commando caterers moves about in silence foldin' an' arrangin' an' tweakin' shit that don't make no realistic sense. Some guys're pilin' weddin' presents in a corner. The crowd spills in every which way breakin' up.

— T'XAAAAAAAY,

Keef. His voice chisels through the noise. Shi'. All I need. I turn around an' spot his squared off ginger head held down makin' a line straigh' for me.

— T'XAAAAY: diamond cunt.

— Keef: football fan. Where'sa Fan Club?

— They're 'ere. They're there. They're comin'. How y'doin'?

— I'm here. Wha' can I tell you?

— You look like piss warmed up.

— I am piss warmed up. I'll be back. I'm bustin'.

I leave Keef standin' an' notice two of his Fan Club headcases laggin' at the door. Nood's right behind me as I head for the toilet.

— Gak. Gakgak. Gakgakgak. Stand in line for a line. Stand in-

— Nood: shut the fuck up an' don't go too far cos I wanna kill ya.

— Sorry 'bou' the drive man. Really I am. Mum had to go somewhere yeah. It was all Stell's idea. She worked it all out on a piece of paper.

— Yeah an' I married Baba.

I take a piss an' feel like sobbin' from relief. Tiredness. Nood's in one of the cubicles chalkin' up some lines on a little chrome plate mirror. After I'm done I go put my arm round him.

— So where would you like to die?

— In the arms of my loved one.

— I was thinkin' more like in here or in there.

— Come on man. Gak gak.

So I do the charlie an' Lendon busts in.

— *Toiletgangsters*. Jus' like old times innit Nood.

— Would be only we ain't doin' evo-stick no more.

Lendon does a line growls a coupla times an' his mug sets in a grimace.

— I flogged most of the gear already Tax, says Nood smilin' at Lendon.

— I'm happy for the both of yous, I say as the line kicks in, but the night is young. Y'na mean. All typsa shit's gonna-

— Don't worry I'm gonna make my speech.

So then Kings an' Baba bust in.

— Guys guys, says Kings. They really should swap around and have the toilet the size of the hall. Who're the assholes outside?

— Leave my mum out of it Kings-

— Nood: I'm talking about the guys wearing England shirts under their suits.

— Oh them guys. Who are they Tax?

— Fuckin' 'ell man you know who: Keef. He's brung along a coupla pavin' slabs from Deptford.

— Yeah them, says Baba. They're eyeballin' me. Y'na mean? I'll twist their fuckin' heads off if they eyeball me. Understand? Cos you know what's next don't you? You know-

— Don't start Baba, says Nood.

— Wha'? What did you say?

— Nah listen up: they pro'ly come for that march innit. I'll talk to Keef, I say.

— Don't talk to 'em says Baba. I wan' 'em out. Cos you know what's next don't you? Hear me Nood? You know what's next.

— I only invited Keef plus one innit. Like his chick. Never figured he'd bring the whole fuckin' away team.

117

— So get rid of them Nood before they start with the monkey nut bullshit.

— Alrigh' Kings no sweat. Tax: Keef can stay. The cuntsa go'a go. Yeah?... I said yeah?

I look at Nood Lend Kings Baba.

— Righ'. Well I'll just throw them out then. Take 'em by the ear an' tell them they go'a go home for their neckties. Simple really. Y'sister could do it.

— Righ' behind ya man, says Lendon laughin'.

An' so they all star' laughin' an' keelin' about as they see my face. An' as I'm out the toilet headed for Keef they're piled up lookin' through the crack in the door. I sift through sayin' hello an' that to Ez Daisy an' people. There's cool beers bein' broken out. I grab one an' just pour down my dry throat. Keef's comin' toward me beckonin' his mates to come with him. They're makin' a big space for themselves. Just comin' through. I go up real close to Keef tryina be confidential.

— Keef Keef look listen-

— Fworgh gi's a lug, says Keef eyein' the beer.

So I give it him.

— Yeah look man a quick word, I say.

— 'Ere T'XAAY meet a coupla me best ones.

— Keef. Kee-

I grab his arm tryina pull him aside but his best ones're already there. They look bad like a coupla suedehead cabbages soaked in lager. Guys like that just don't give a fuck. They got nothin' to live for.

— This 'ere's T'XAAAY. An' this 'ere's my mate Numma Eleven an' my uvver mate Big Numma Five. Y'shoulda come out wiv us Saturday nigh' Tax. Went down Stallions in Peckham.

— Yeah? Listen Keef-

— Saw me ex down there wiv her cunt boyfriend. I told him I's givin' her beans before him so he calls me a cunt an' we had a scrap. Give him a righ' mullerin' so she's back with me now. You slippin' anyone the old fish?

— Nah... Listen Keef...

I glance about. People movin' an' laughin'. Jace an' Daise rappin' out P-Funk in a corner: *Make my funk the Nood funk... I want my funk uncut...* Can't see no back-up available. I'm figurin' Keef's best ones've got some homemade tools in their armpits. Only takes a second an' they're gone. Keef's rollin' his eyes about grinnin' just waitin for a punchline to laugh to.

— Keef: I go'a tell ya man... the guys... they go'a go.

— Eh?

— They ain't invited na mean. Nood don't know 'em. Na mean. Na'm sayin'...

— Wha'? says Keef when he sees I mean it. Whassis fuckin'... You're tellin' me my mates they go'a go?

— Thassi'.

— Fuckin' 'ell. 'Oo sez? Come all this fuckin' way. Fuckin'... Where's Nood then?

— Listen man he's busy with the family an' shit. Says he's real sorry. Na mean. Way it is.

— Cunt's takin' the fuckin' piss. Fuckin'-

— Ain't you Keef na'm sayin'...

Keef screws his face like he's doin' a maths exam. He's finkin': *one way it's bloodshed. Uvver way it ain't.* But before he can figure the problem Big Numma Five moves into space. He leans in over me an inch from my face reekin' of Old Spiss.

— Too many fuckin' coons anyway. Look at them coon bitches.

Numma Eleven lights up like he was programmed.

— Black bastards.

— Yeah they're everywhere innit, I say. Coons yids spics micks dicks you name it they're here. Alrigh'?

— Nah it fuckin' ain't. You tell Nood he ain't heard the last of it. No: better still get the cunt over. I don't fuckin' talk to go-betweens an' you can tell him that from me.

I dunno what the fuck to do. I know I have to face them down here an' now but I also know the two Nummas probably brung their own body bags. Victory or death innit. Sit tight for the cavalry. I know they go'a appear. Just a matter of before or after I'm dead is all.

— You gonna get the cunt or wha'?

— Ain't gettin' him Keef I told ya.

Then I see Baba siftin' through the crowd behind them. Keef ain't got the heart for a scrap but he ain't gonna lose face in front of his mates. So Keef an' me're eyeballin' each other for the benefit of two fuckheads. Then the guys half emerge out the crowd like not before time an' surround them. I guess Keef can see the relief in my face. I ain't got the heart for it either. I mean the wild west ain't exactly gonna impress Char.

But thing is Numma Five's slow to pick up the new situation. Down by his waist he punches his palm his face seized ugly with hate:

— Say the word Keef I'll do the cunt...

Keef could say somethin' either way but he don't.

— Come on just say the word sss-

The rest just comes out Big Numma Five's mouth in one long *sssss* cos Baba grabs him under the ribs from behind. For a long moment everyone's listenin' to the air comin' out of his gut as he folds slow an' watchin' his eyeballs to see if they're gonna pop. He's droolin' out his wide open gob tongue flappin' as Baba carries him to the door. Numma Eleven's too shitted to move. It's like everyone knows there ain't nothin' to be done. We watch them go an' they're through the door before anyone reacts. Nood turns to Keef.

— Told you not to bring 'em along.

— Ain't lookin' for a scrap Nood. S'posed to be a weddin'. Ain't lookin'-

— Outside Keef.

We escort them out the place in silence. An' I know what it's gonna be out there. Round the side of the Slice there's an alley. It's cobbled all the way along. Quiet. No traffic. In the late sun buzzin' with insects it could be a country lane. Could be a place where the spill out from the Slice just kick back to smoke an' take in the air. Whatever.

Twenty feet down it Numma Five's lyin' on the floor holdin' his mouth. There's blood runnin' all over his England shirt then drippin' on the floor an' mixin' with diesel an' grit between the cobbles. Baba's squattin' over him cleanin' off his blade on a clean bit of shirt.

— Next...

I'm lookin' round for Kings an' Nood. But they both got this look in their faces like that's that: Baba's out his box an' he's gonna do what he's gonna do. It's like I can hear inside everyone's head. Nobody wants it but it's gonna happen. You just have to be cool til it's over. Hang back til goin' home time comes round. After that it's easy. After that or tomorrow or the next day we can all say the fuckheads had it comin'. An' all of us will say that. An' it'll be the truth. Then there'll be the jokes. The big talk. An' all of us'll pull together bustin' our guts laughin' cos we're in it together an' it'll all move on one step nearer to the night.

— Baba le'm go man.

This comes out my mouth like a whisper like a voice that ain't even mine. Baba's still hunched but he turns his head lookin' at me with a single eye.

— I said next.

Koom an' a guy called Wes shove Numma Eleven forward. He tries to punch out but his legs're jelly. His fists just flail about useless like he was catchin' flies. He gets shoved round from Koom to Wes an' from Joey to Kings an' back.

— Dey's like the guys what done us innit Joey, says Koom.

— Fifteen twenny of 'em man. Fuckin' nazi skins. Didn't stand no fuckin' chance. Do it Baba. Cut his fuckin' lip off.

That's it. They all got a fuckin' cause now. Numma Eleven gets punched down on the floor like it was nothin'. He don't even squeak. Baba cuts his lip an' we all start to go back inside leavin' Keef starin' at his shoes. There's blood seepin' round them. Everyone looks at it as they pass an' gets a rush. Proof that something's happened. A big thing.

Koom an' Joey're mouthin' off about how they tried to fight off this nazi army an' Baba's gettin' slapped on the back. Inside there's noise an' music. Zeb an' Ez've got some corny duo goin' on a piano in one corner with Shitsky jammin' along. Stell's broads're kickin' out in sync like a chorus line. Stell herself's organisin' people at the tables an' makin' sure they's all sorted for places.

But they all look up when this band of guys come back in. Everyone's joshin' an' posin' in the limelight biggin' up their lives like they was auditionin' for cockrocker of the year. Like they ain't never satisfied with who they are an' always have to be like someone else who's bigger an' better. An' Nood's way out front blindin' himself. He's star of the whole show. He's top banana. His people. His big day. His fuckin' night.

— NOOOD, Stell's shoutin' across the hall, ge'm sat down. Grub's comin'.

— Ain't made me speech yet babes, Nood shouts back.

— Wait til after.

— Don't gimme no lip babes, says Nood pointin' at Stell but lookin' at the guys.

Everybody creases up includin' most of them that don't even know the score. But the guys're reactin' like it's the joke of the week.

— He give you lip? says Lendon.

— Nah I give *him* lip, says Baba.

— But Numma Eleven give *me* lip, says Joey.

— You give him lip back? says Koom.

— I give him his lip back, says Baba.

— Flippin' lip lopped innit, says Nood.

An' so on. The whole time I'm siftin'. Always behind whoever's talkin'. Never lookin' at no one long enough to say shit. We move to the tables with Stell on carnival traffic duty. Way she's worked it out there's a head table with her Nood an' the mums. Then one table for Nood's family an' cousins one for Stell's an' a third mainly for the guys. Probably the smartest thing she done.

As table number three's gettin' sorted I'm checkin' in all the faces. Ringers burglars teefs filches dips an' deedees. Scammers an' skankers. Specialist form-fillers an' *loophole* operators. *Businessmen.* Clever muggers an' at least a coupla of full time bastards who musta popped out their mothers' screamin' holes with knives ready in their hands. An' then a few that's just watched too much tv. But everybody's somebody. I'm sat with them. So I must be too.

— Alrigh' everyone, Nood's shoutin'.

The place goes a bit quiet an' Nood looks round just surveyin' it all. Cunt looks at practically every face in turn. Keeps his eye lingerin' just a bit longer'n anyone can handle. Like in the end even Baba can't look him straight back. In fact most of the faces on table three're screwed up. There's plates of steamin' puke an' spuds in gravy with some sad fuckin' sausages pokin' out. Like school dinners that nobody on table three's gonna eat 'part from Baba. An' him an' the charlie've killed my appetite anyhow.

— Jus' wanna say a few words of thanks an' that before we get stuck in...

— Crank it up, someone shouts.

— Yeah alrigh' alrigh', says Nood louder, ...Wanna say thanks to me mum an' Stell's mum... Carole on the left an' Marion here on the righ'... for bein' there *one hundred per cent all the way*.

They get a round of applause an' look at each other embarrassed.

— An' that goes for the rest of all the families an' that for turnin' up... even if I did forget your birthdays... Special big thank you as well to all the scumpigs. They know who they are. Specially them what's on the tick list. An' another thing...

Nood points to the corner where there's a pile of video recorders a coupla portable teles a karaoke an' a loada electric nonsense such as food blenders.

— ...you coulda checked with each other before you went out an' nicked the same gear na mean...

The suspects love that one. They're smilin' wise at each other. Everybody else loves it too. Now they're all in on some real naughty secret. They all know people now. They'll all be tellin' stories in whispers to their friends that begin with *I know this guy right*...

— Whass wrong wiv a bi'a shrinkage anyway? Car boot job innit, Ez's shoutin' over the din.

— Not like they aggrava'ed no one in their own home is it, adds Deez in what he thinks is a normal voice but which makes all the forks vibrate.

The place fades down to silence.

— Well thanks for them comments but stick to what you know boys: *frontloadin'*. Na mean...

More stupid laughin'. Nood takes a sigh.

— Last- at long bloody last- I wanna say thanks to me best man Tax. He was gonna make a speech about me but he couldn't think of nothin' sweet to say...

There's a load of clappin' for that gag. I find myself laughin' along hot an' embarrassed. An' Nood ain't even done.

— ...So I'm gonna tell a little thing 'bou' him instead...

More clappin'. Fuckin' Nood. I got nowhere to look but down.

— ...Tax righ' is workin' with this other guy Stylianou in this little cinema whass now closed down. Which won't come as no surprise after you hear this. The cinema's got this righ' little hitler runnin' the show always givin' both of 'em heavy pressure an' shit wage. Only he ain't around too much... So Tax an' Stylianou righ' they star' doin' a little cookin'...

— Gaaaa y'na mean...

Nood nods scannin' about cos all faces're on him. All except mine tha' is. I dunno where the fuck not to look.

— So wha' they do? says Koom.

— I's comin' to tha' in a jiffy... Wha' they do is this: they start sellin' the cinema tickets like usual to whoever come in. Bu' then instead of tearin' 'em in half down at the entrance they take 'em back whole. An' then they sell the *same* ones again to the *new* punters whass comin' in...

— Tasty, goes Lendon thinkin' through the balance sheet.

— Na mean. Only course by the end o' the night it looks like hardly any bastard tickets've been flogged. An' this goes on week in week out. *Subtle* at first na mean. Hitler don't really twig. He just get a dose of *slow panic*... An' it builds up in him an' keeps on buildin'. By the end he's doin' his fuckin' nut cos he's gettin' pressure from higher up. They wanna know why the take is so cak an' why even James Bond on a Saturday night's only got two punters. An' one of *them's* James's mum na mean... 'Ventually hitler's go'a blame i' all somewhere even if he can't figure out whass happenin'. So one day he calls Tax an' Stylianou over an' tells 'em he's got new people an' that's that they're both fired. Stylianou don't care. He's well down with that an's walkin' ou' the door straigh' away no questions countin' his extra peas. But Tax don't follow. He turns to hitler. An' wha' d'y'reckon he does?

— NUTS HIM, screams li'l Joey.

— Sees hitler's sister, says Ez.

— *Torches* the gaff, says Lendon.

— No. You're all totally wrong. Tax goes: *ain't you gonna ask abou' the money then?*

— Oh ma god, says Koom, shut up. He don't... Hey Tax-

— Wait wait wait. So hitler goes *I don't care about the fuckin' money. It ain't mine anyway.*

— So den wha'? goes Koom.

— So then Tax looks him square an' goes: *well if it ain't yours I don't fuckin' want it.* Then Tax takes out a loada dough thass a wedge even if it ain't the whole deal... an' guess wha': *he gives it back.*

There's this jaw-droppin' moment of silence round the hall broken by Koom's shakin' voice:

— NO. No. Tell me it ain't so.

People crack up either laughin' at me or with me but they're laughin'. They're all shoutin' for me to finish it. To say the final word. To say in my own words why I did what I did.

— Ah don't ge' i'. I' don' make no sense, Koom's shoutin', Why d'ya give the money back to hitler jus' cos it wasn't his to steal?

Nood points to me an' they all fall quiet. Fuckin' Nood.

— Thass the point, I say to Koom, knowin' i' wasn't his just took the joy out of stealin' it.

— An' that's why he's my driver ladies an' gents: cos he's in it for the *LIFESTYLE* . Na mean.

Now that's a thing they can all find funny in the same fuckin' way. An' they do. They clap. An' I can hear bits of the story repeatin' round the place an' people laughin' again an' makin' comments. I can't help lookin' over at Charmaine who's with the rest of Nood's family. She's lookin' at me like she knows all about me. Like she really cares. She makes me sick. I make myself sick. My palms're sweated up. I look down at the gravy on my plate. There's spots of grease floatin' an' breakin' up into rainbow colours. Blood an' oil. Nood's hushin' 'em down an' pullin' Stell up off her feet.

— One last thing: I go'a say thanks to Stell innit. None o' this would be happenin' if she hadn't said yes.

— I didn't say yes. You did. An' it wasn't yes. More like *yeah alrigh'*. Innit.

— Yeah well whatever someone had to say it. Na mean babes.

More laughter. Nood can't put a foot wrong.

— Anyway. Got a little announcement here. Get ready mum: me an' Stell... I mean Stell she's in the family way...

Both mums almost pass out into their spuds but by now there's yelpin' an' cheerin'. Nood's shoutin' high above the din.

— It's all legit. Totally legit. We're hitched.

I look at Lendon opposite. He nods at me dead serious. I see the back of the car covered in baby shit an' nappies. Stell an' Nood're down each other's throats with Stell's ass headin' for the gravy on her plate. Some of the guys start a slow hand clap that catches on round the tables. 'Ventually they disentangle their clinch. Nood gives his mouth a rock an' roll wipe.

— Alrigh' everyone... Let the disco begin...

Around the hall people're tuckin' in. There's crates of beer an' bottles of wine bein' passed up an' down. Baba's sat next to me slurpin' down the sausages. On the other side of me's Jace. She's got a chain from her ear to her nose ring an' a stud in her lip. She's already sparked up a cigarette an' is givin' Lendon the eye. They're about to compare rings on their fingers. Rest of the table's breakin' up into arguments. Least Baba don't expect me to talk about the weather. But I'm gettin' the fear just listenin' to him chew. Fuck am I doin'. Like I'm train surfin'. Out of control just hangin' on for the whole ride. When I's a kid it was a wicked buzz. Ambushin' some train on the network an' ridin' it wherever. But it's like I just been waitin' to fall off my whole stanky life.

— No appetite? says Baba lookin' my plate over.

— All yours, I say slidin' it toward him.

I start to get up an' catch sight of Keef comin' back in. He's got his hands in his pockets just to show he ain't seekin' revenge. But he's grinnin' at me like we was separated at birth.

— T'XAAAAAY.

— Keef...

— T'XAAY, says Keef puttin' his arm round me. Diamond cunt. Jus' give Nood a quick hallo. Back in a mo'.

I look down at Baba. He shrugs.

— Guess he saw the light, he says pullin' a fork out his mouth.

I sit back down an' watch as Keef slaps Nood on the back. He congratulates him on his weddin' like nothin' happened. An' Nood don't mind his ass gettin' licked in public. Keef comes back over pullin' up a chair an' starin' down Jace's front.

— Ain't seen you in years Jace. Can see you filled out y'forms correctly though.

Jace half smiles but her an' Lendon're practically sniffin' each other by now. Keef sticks out his hand to Baba. Baba sort of knows the hand's there to shake but there's no way he's gonna so much as look at it. Baba just carries on moppin' up them sausages listenin' to some row about music between Ezra an' Shitsky at the other end of the table.

— Your fokkin sounds stink man, Shitsky's shoutin'. Whass dis *grongee* shit man.

— It's grunge you cunt. Grunge metal... Fuckin' 'ell you wouldn't know tecno from garage. You think hip hop's medication for one legged grandmas na mean.

Most of the table's kinda bein' drawn in to this discussion an' furniture's shiftin' down with people takin' sides. Keef's been fidgetin' next to me. He's got these bushy orange eyebrows he keeps scratchin' with his chewed up middle finger. There's somethin' about a habit like that. Makes my stomach clench up. He leans in close.

— Jus' private like Tax... 'tween you an' me... cos we go back a ways an' that... I coulda sorted that. You know... before... what happened an' that. I woulda... you know... sorted it. No problem. Piece o' piss. Piece o' fuckin' piss. You know... You know... Jus' wen' abou' i' the wrong fuckin' way didn' I. Know mean. Wrong fuckin' approach. Didn't think it all through. Thass i' innit. Wasn't time really innit. Y'know'm sayin'. Story o' me life that. Coulda made a fuckin' goldmine...

— But I s'pose you went about it the wrong way...

— Thass it. Thass righ'. Did eighteen months Brixton didn't I.

— An' that was jus' the last time.

— Yeah well... you go'a keep perseverin'. Crime pays innit.

— Not in your case boy.

— Nah... but...

— But what?

— Pay in the end though won't it.

— If you say so. Jus' don't give up the day job na mean.

Keef sparks up reflectin' on these words of wisdom. He's got his head up his ass. Half hour ago he'da been all set to go Banglabashin' down Brick Lane with the Fan Club. Now he's back with the guys like he knows the score. Koom comes over with some beers.

— Gaaaa: so wha'ppen to the Nummas Keef?

— Drove 'emselves to casualty innit, says Keef openin' a beer. Fuck 'em I say.

— No hard feelins only dey was a coupla cunts you was wiv innit.

— Thass why I ain't down there givin' 'em blow jobs to take the pain away.

— Gaaaa. You're alrigh' Keef. Inn'e Tax.

— Keef's one of the guys. Always was always will be.

— Thass righ', says Keef. Thass righ'...

I'm wonderin' what Baba woulda meted out if Keef'd been in competition. Or stolen his money. I try to catch Nood's attention but he's havin' a go at one of the caterers.

— Tarte- cherrie- glacée: fuck'sat? Eh? Ain't even fresh. I was told it'd be apple pie or rhubarb.

— I'm afraid we-

— Wha'?

— It's alright Stevie. It looks fine. It'll be fine don't worry. Straight from the box.

— Mum do I look like a *boil in the bag* sor'a bloke? Don't answer.

Nood shoves a chair out the way an' comes toward us straightenin' his tie well pissed off.

— Koom. A word yeah, he says glancin' at me without stoppin'.

Koom traipses off after him to the toilet. After a bit I follow knowin' loadsa people's clockin' this activity. By the time I'm in Nood's crowdin' Koom.

— Wha' can Ah say Nood?

— Don't have to say nothin'. Jus' give us the six fifty.

— Dass wha' Ah'm tellin' ya man: it's der bu' i' ain't.

— *It's der bu' i' ain't* ?

— Y'na mean.

— Lemme get this straigh': it's there... but it ain't not there. Thass righ' innit Tax?

— Yeah righ', I say floppin' down on a toilet seat, it *is* there. Bu' it is not there.

I start billin' up a little spliff of leb. Nood gives his hands a quick wash an' examines his nails. Then the smoothness of his chin. Then seems to check a partin' in his hair which he ain't got. Then his ears for wax. Which he has got. Finally he turns to Koom again.

— So where the fuck is it?

— Wha' can Ah say Nood?

— Give us fuckin' three hundred an' I'll tick the rest til the end of the week. Fair enough innit. Fair motherfucker I am. Na mean.

— Yeah yeah iss fair—

— But it ain't? DON' MESS ME—

— Ah ain't Nood. We got stung innit. Nazis took us innit. What can Ah do? We got hided. What can Ah—

Nood prods him in the chest an' keeps proddin' til Koom's leanin' backward against one of the wash basins.

— I don't normally hit blokes whass wearin' bandages...

— Ah ain't go' it. Ah jus' ain't. If Ah had it Ah'd give it ya.

— Get it off y'mum I don't care.

— Well she don't work in the silver spoon factory no more. What can Ah say?

— You're excruciatin' me on my weddin' day you fuckhead. With your smart fuckin' answers. Na mean. I'll kick y'fuckin' arse til y'nose bleeds. Cunt.

The toilet door opens as I figured it was gonna sooner or later. Kings an' Baba's heads appear like two halves of one asshole.

— I might've guessed, says Kings lookin' at Baba.

— Like the godfather inn'e, says Baba.

Nood's about to say somethin' but Kingsley waves a ringed finger in his face.

— No no Nood hang on lemme guess... Koom owes you a pile but because of some bizarre planetary movement the money's trapped in the twilight zone.

— Yeah unless it's rolled up in his bandage, says Nood.

— It ain't der. An' it ain't in no twiligh' zone neeva.

— Wha'm I supposed to do with this cunt Kings? Tell me that.

— I was about to, says Kings with a grade one charm school smile. How much d'you owe him Koom?

— Thass between—

— He's askin' you how much, says Baba.

Baba glances over at me. I can feel I'm aggravatin' him cos I'm not standin' up payin' due respect.

— Six fifty... Six hundred fifty...

— An' how much do you owe us Nood?

— What's that go'a do with it?

— 'Bout fifteen hundred isn't it. Cos the way I see it is this: Koom you don't owe Nood you owe me plus fifty per cent emergency bail out charge. An' Nood: you now owe me eight fifty plus standard interest for late payment. Go dutch on a calculator boys. You got seven days.

Now this is what I call a no bullshit stiffin'. Koom an' Nood're tryina get used to this new picture fast as they can which ain't fast enough. I religh' my spliff an' pass it to Baba like to ease the situation off.

— What the fuck're you doin'? says Baba to me. How come you ain't out there with your nazi lover?

— He ain't no fuckin' friend of mine Baba. You know that.

— Yeah? Well-

— Baba: I'm ready to sort you out here an' now, says Nood.

He takes the money we got off of Eddie an' Gillian out a plastic bag down his trousers an' counts it. There's a kinda *hoomour* in payin' Kings an' Baba off with what was supposed to be their own dollars. Only it means my split don't amount to bus fare.

— Deal or steal innit Koom.

— Yeah Nood: I steal you deal an' them they deal *and* steal innit.

Baba don't know whether to like that remark or hang Koom by his balls. He takes the spliff off me an' passes it to Koom. Koom's uncertain but figures he's go'a accept it. As he reaches for it Baba smacks him in the nose. Not hard but enough to get his nose goin'. Rest of them all start laughin'. An' I laugh too. Can't help myself.

— That's a Kray brothers move, says Baba passin' the spliff back to me.

— Didn't haveta test it out on me. Na mean. It was a joke, says Koom hunchin' up over the basin with blood seepin' out his bandage.

— Personally I thought it was funny, says Kings pattin' him on the back. We deal *and* steal. I like it. That was funny Koom... Not funny Bab?

— Yeah...

Baba raises his eyebrows which is a big deal for him.

— ...Sure... now you mention it it was yeah... Now you owe us Koom I'll be lookin' out for you. I like a guy who can make me laugh...

Baba shrugs his jacket an' makes sure his beard his tie his tie pin his bracelet watch his cufflinks an' his cock're still in place. When he's satisfied everythin's just where it ought to be he looks me an' Nood over. Real careful. Inch by inch. Button at a time. Specially my suit.

— Don't look any better in your steppin' out garms. Like you're going to a funeral. Innit...

— Maybe I am, I say tryina sound big or tricky or I don't know.

They're just the first words that come in my head. Which in this case ain't the best ones. It's no use eyeballin' Baba an' even if it was I mean why the fuck would I. So I just stand there knowin' he ain't doin' nothin' but eyeballin' me. Knowin' like every mug knows least once in his life that *som'in's about to give*.

— Hey joker: what the fuck's that mean?

— Alright Baba, says Kings. You can go now Tax. Got some turkey to talk with Nood.

I look at Nood but his eyes drop to the tile floor for a second like he's just seen the contact lens he's been searchin' for. Like the whole situation's gonna pass through his system an' out like beer. Like he's gonna come back absent-minded sayin' *sorry guys where were we?* Trouble is there's this silence. Long or short who gives a fuck it's big an' fat. An' it tells everyone he's beat.

— Anything you go'a say you can say in front of him, says Nood about as convincin' as a guy with a bloody nose.

I shoulda walked. Just walked. Just started whenever an' however an' kept on.

— Listen to him, says Baba. What you want him around for Nood? Tax ain't gonna do nothing for you. He's pussy...

Baba leans in over me noddin' right in my face.

— ...Innit. Innit Tax. Batty boy. *Oh Baba let them go man please let them go oh please Baba please*. Innit. Eh?

— Gaaaaaa.

They all laugh includin' Nood even though he knows he's about to get crowded.

— Go keep an eye for Marcello Tax...

I stand there a second without movin'.

— Well go on then, says Nood like he's back in the seat, I don't want no fuckin' nonsense. Righ'. No fuckin' shit Tax. Understand?

— Roger Nood... Guys...

I smile at Baba's big joke an' nod an' keep my cool but come out the toilet worse off than when I went in. Which ain't supposed to be the way with toilets. Nood should be squeezin' people. Sussin' out the future. 'Stead he's gettin' squeezed left an' righ'. Walkin' into every hole like a fuckin' sap. 'Ventually he's gonna take it bendin' over like the rest of the fuckin' saps. An' he'll sell anyone along the way. Starts me wonderin' about Lendon.

Back in the hall they're all well juiced up. Everyone's findin' their groove for the evenin'. Elly an' Stell've got their arms linked an're singin' *Pretty Woman* on the karaoke with an' audience slowhandin' along. Mannie's kid's bustin' bottles into a metal dustbin. Lendon an' Jace're suckfacin' by the fag machine. An' Shitsky an' co've got some gamblin' goin' on a backgammon board with a bunch of guys smokin' down skunk coughin' their guts out an' disputin'.

— ACEY FOKKIN' DOOCEY. I'M CLEANIN' OP MUDDERS.

— FOKK YOU TOKKIN ABOUT, Shuddupsky shouts. What you need sucker is sweet DOBBLE SIXES...

— Pony all round. Here i' comes, says Deez throwin' the dice.

Everyone tracks the cubes ready to grab for the bills.

— YAAAAAH. SIXAAHS... Y'MUTHAFUCKAS...

Nine oh four an' thirty seconds

I sift through slowly toward the street exit pickin' up a beer on the way. Outside the traffic's died off. I notice Vijay an' Eamm further up in the bend of Kilburn Lane. They're silently offloadin' cardboard boxes from Vijay's transit into the boot of Eamm's car. Dead serious like they was on a government mission. After a coupla dozen they finish up an' both repark outside the Slice. Vijay hops out his van givin' his tache a comb an' liftin' out a small box. Vijay's one of those guys just can't keep still. Always practisin' steps pullin' up his baggy jeans an' checkin' his feet.

— How y'doin' man, he says with Eamm comin' up behind him.

— Laggin'.

— Safe... Wha're the chicks like in there?

— Dynamite. You ain't got enough eyes.

— Oh yeah? Like Nood's a real woman's man. They jus' sor'a *cling* to him innit.

— Nah, says Eamm, they get drawn in. Lifestyle issue innit. They jus' sort of *have* to come to him.

— Yeah by post, says Veej. Argos catalogue. Twenny four ninety nine with a dozen coupons.

— 'Cept for one of 'em, says Eamm flippin' his wrist so's his thumb slaps.

— Who's that then?

— I think Eamm's referrin' to Charmaine.

— Lendon's sister, says Eamm with this low growl. Bitch is well slack.

— WHOA man, says Veej makin' like he's gonna pass out, Lendon's sister? Gotta be fucked in the head givin' her a squeeze. 'Sides she is *ugly* in the face man.

— Nah she ain't, I say.

— *Listen* to stud. I tell you for free man: you'll catch some genetic thing offa her. End up like Lendon. Armed an' dangerous. Only with him it's armed an' *confused*. You know. Mess with his sister...

Veej cocks his hand like a gun at my head.

— ...BAM. Game over. Na mean.

I look at him blank. An' Eamm don't look wiser.

— Yeah man. Lend's packin' heat. He's packin' a rod. Iron. Fill you fulla lead. BAM BAAM muthafucka.

Eamm sor'a laughs. Neither of us know if he's really serious.

— Wha'm I talkin'? Hebrew Hindi Horseshit wha'? I'm talkin' pure *no* shit. He showed it me. Wicked fuckin' piece. Handgun. Personal protection system. WHOA I say: do not approach. Hey listen Tax-

— Lendon's got a gun? I mumble.

— Wha'd I just say? Lissen-

Vijay puts his arm on my shoulder an' I feel a pitch comin' on.

— ...I got some serious fuckin' product I know y'gonna relish. Reeboks. Five-oh a pair. Real thing man. One fifty plus in the shops. Durability guaranteed. Take a look...

— Nah man...

— What no? Jus' take a look at these...

Vijay opens the box under my nose lookin' at me like he knows the contents'll blow me away. But he sees I ain't impressed.

— Turbo charged triple stitched scientific air compression system. Fifty to you.

— Nah... Ain't runnin' no more man.

— Stand an' streetfight innit, says Eamm laughin'. Is what they're for anyway. Or burglin'...

— 'Xactly wha'm sayin' Eamm. Essential an' crucial an' all that to y'overall image that you wanna put out on the S-T-R-double E-big T.

— Yeah but Veej I give up my image way back.

— I can tell. Shi' man but you go'a look good for your crew. How 'bou' some Nike? Fila? Air Jordan import? What you after? Must want som'in man. Name it. Name y'game. Sort you out some fuckin' Armani for the weekend.

— Next time man.

— *Next* time he says. Ain't gonna be no next time man. This is now. Wha' 'bout some gold? Gold chains man you go'a have y'gold. Lighters? Clippers. Box of a hundred a score. Is that a deal or wha'?

— Lissen to the guy, Eamm laughs. Fuckin' bhangramuffin attitood there.

— Product gangstas kick ass innit.

— Not this ass man. But there's punters queuin' for your magic inside. An' mega stakes on backgammon. Wicked prizes... assault rifles... teenage girls...

This gets the two of them excited an' they straighten up. Vijay tries a parting shot.

— Do you two pairs Reeboks - *your selection* - fifteen. No pressure. Free mystery gift. Sale of the freakin' century. Talk to me.

— Get a life.

— Get a knife more like. Fuuuuck. I'm out.

They disappear inside with Eamm laughin' an' Veej cussin' all over. I sit down on the step to catch some of the dyin' rays. Two doors up the lights in the Golden Temple takeaway come on. Yellow neon on red sky. A family car rolls up an' the dad gets out. Big bald in a tight t-shirt. Just another bloke with car keys swingin'. The rest're all sat there in silence. Two vegetable kids peerin' into nowhere through the space between the front seats. Their mum focused on the windscreen. All waitin' for their fix of stir fry an' video like smackheads.

I should be back in there. In the middle of the crowd. Right in there with all of them. Always feelin' for the dead centre. Movin' with it. Watchin' it. Doin' what it does. Cos crowds can turn. They have a way of turnin' inside out leavin' the middle on the edge. Can happen a hundred time a night but you just haveta keep crawlin' back. Like Keef. Stayin' there in the middle. Ready to turn when it turns. Paddlin' long as you can. Grabbin' whatever you can. Cos there's nowhere an' nobody else.

The dad comes back with the food. I get a whiff of warm paper bag. Before gettin' in he orders one of the kids out with a flick of his finger. The kid gets out not darin' to look up.

— Pickled onion. I want change out of that, says dad flippin' a fifty pee onto the pavement.

The kid bends down to pick it up. Goes into the Golden Temple big scared eyes chin down an' after a bit comes out with a little bag. Dad gets out again to let him in. He can see the kid just wants to get back in the car. So he puts a leg in his way.

— Where's my change? Eh? How much d'I give you? Come on: how much?

— Fifty pee.

— Did I give you fifty pee y'little bastard?

— You-

— Shut it, says dad snatchin' the bag.

He leans right down to his son's face. The kid can probably smell thirty a day an' a barrel of beer on him. He's probably holdin' his breath not to smell that smell that's already on his clothes in his hair an' on his pillow at night.

— How much d'I give you? Come on how much? Is that all the change. Five pee...

He smiles like he's enjoyin' it. Like his world's all arranged the way he wants. Just a matter of which channel to watch: comedy or action. Then the smile washes out.

— I give you a pound. Tellin' me a pickled onion cost you ninety five...

The kid says something but I can't hear.

— Wha'? Answer me when I'm fuckin' talkin' to you. Pull a flanker an' you know what you'll get.

— It was fifty. It was...

Dad stands to his full height. The kid freezes lookin' ahead at what must look like a wall of gut. Dad transfers the onion bag to his left hand. He waits like he's figurin' angles. An' the kid waits cos there's nothin' else he can do. Except maybe count the holes on dad's belt. Then when the time is just right when the kid's face is turnin' to look at the shinin' right palm... that's when he lets one go. Open hand. It's the callusy part under his fingers that connects with the kid's face an' sends him to the floor.

Then he dumps the kid seat of the pants back in the car an' starts whackin' shit out of him so's the car's rockin'. Mum looks out a sidewindow. On the other side of the junction Ladbroke Grove snakes over the bridge to West London. It's like I can hear the crap in the sewers bubblin' an' feedin' the stink above. I feel like jumpin' out this whole thing only it wouldn't look too good. An' the thing'd follow me to the edge of the M25 an' drag me back by the balls.

Must be ten

It's already dark by the time Marcello's lambretta comes farting round the corner with Steffi on the back like in some sixties movie. Only Marcello's in the seventies tonight with his snakeskin shoes flared check trousers batwing collar an' peardrop mirror shades. An' Steff's garmed up for a disco inferno. The front wheel hits the pavement an' lurches up onto it. Probably cos Marcello can't see a fuckin' thing. Almost takes my foot with it. They get off grinnin'. So I grin back.

— Where is de rave? says Marcello takin' off his dayglo green bone dome.

— Cancelled mate. Try again tomorrow.

— You are making a joke I hopp because Iyama ready to powder de nose and to boogie.

— Right on bro'.

I look at Steff tryina to catch her eye but she's primpin' up her silver glitter hair in a window. When she turns I stand up an' go to kiss her on the cheeks but our noses collide. I try an' laugh it off. She comes out of it a lot worse with her eyes waterin'. I try laughin' that off too.

Marcello's already dancin' about practisin' a James Brown shuffle on one foot. Same time he flashes his shades on an' off givin' out insane stares like he's on a charlie bender. Which I guess he is.

— Leada de way, he says pushin' past into the Slice.

I feel someone's got to warn him about the general state of things. But I don't want anythin' taken down an' used in evidence. So I let Steffi go ahead an' hang back to collect the porn out the boot. I go over to the car an' open up.

The boot light comes on in the dark reflectin' off of the glossy magazines. There's a reader's wife grinnin' pink nipple at me. I get a grip with both hands under the box but notice right next to it the wheel jack. Rusty. Chipped black. Maybe the moon's full bu' I just get some kinda notion an' take the jack out an' put it in the nearest street bin coverin' it with half a newspaper. Then I go back take out the box an' elbow the boot shut. The box weighs a ton like I's carryin' a coffin with the souls of ten thousand sad fuckers inside.

On my way back I stop at the door of the Slice. It's got *private function* taped across one cracked glass panel. Red green lights flash from inside. I can hear Zeb's voice amplified through the PA boomin' like the voice of god with added reverb.

— NUFF RESPECT IN THE HOUSE OUSE OUSE... MC ZEB D PLAYS A LIQUID SELECTION SHUN SHUN SHUN...

I know the whole fuckin' selection. I should know it by now. My fingers press on the swing door. As it opens a coupla inches Nood's mug is confrontin' me. It's lifeless like he's just parked it at the door an' gone for a piss. He looks through me. An' me through him. Then we're both surprised to see each other. Like we been caught off guard lookin' through the drugs that've twisted up our faces an' then through the twists. An' there ain't nothin' between us except the twists. Nood's been makin' deals I don't wanna know about.

— You got ple- ple- plenty o' cunt in 'ere mate, I say to break it.

Nood looks down into the box withou' movin' his head.

— Give a dog a bone.

We crease up. But somehow we ain't laughin'. I pass him the box an' we go in. Steff's dancin' in front of Ez with her arms in the air. Marcello's cleared a big space around him with some fucked up breakdance that leaves him lurchin' after the spins. His trousers've slipped down under his belly an' his crack's showin'. Family people've taken cover in a group with the remains of the food. Everyone else has settled down to the chaos.

Nood goes over to the barman Joe the Eye an' nods toward the office. Joe's old busted face comes alive an' his lazy eye shifts around the place like a searchlight. I catch a glimpse of Baba givin' Char the talk in a distant corner. We slip into the office behind the bar.

It's dusty an' steamin' in there no more than a corridor with rows of shelves both sides. Desk an' filin' cabinet at the end. The desk's stacked high with papers an' invoices. Joe sweeps the loose ones into a pile an' stuffs them into the cabinet. Nood takes a box of Joe's Irish folk tapes off the chair an' slumps into it.

— Shall I be mother? he says takin' out the charlie.

— Long as I don't got t' impregnate you in any way whatsoever, says Joe laughin'.

Nood starts chalkin' a few lines out on the desktop includin' a real fat one for Joe. Joe watches while I pull a few pages out of one of the magazines. I tear a square through some naked body an' crease out the first wrap.

Joe starts conductin' himself through some song about sweet Mary from Galway an' snorts up a six inch line instead of the chorus. His whole face turns white then sweaty red.

— Nood you're a fockin' star a real fockin' starrrrr. I'll be gettin' back t' the porveyin' o' liquor...

— Joe do us a favour yeah: get Marcello in here.

— Which one's Mar- RAAACHOO... Ah... 'scuse me..., says Joe givin' his nose a wipe. Which one's Marcello?

— The guy clearin' the dance floor with his ass hangin' out. Can't miss him, I say.

Joe starts to back out the door cos there ain't room to turn. His lazy eye scans across the box of porn.

— Hey Nood: you discovered *goirls* or som'in?

— They're for you Joe: quality used mags. Bargain. If you want 'em...

— Well I got no moral objection...

We all have to laugh at this like buddies. Joe backs out closin' the door behind him. After givin' his head a good scratch so's hair an' flake an' shit's revolvin' in the air Nood chalks us out some skinnier lines. In silence. His head's down over the desk concentratin' on powderisin' lumps of coke. His neck's bare. When you see someone like that you can't help thinkin' how easy it is for them to die. With me it's ways of killin' him goin' through my head. Knives razors axes piano wire. Then I could cut him up into handy bits an' file him in the cabinet.

Nood rolls a note does his lines then passes the note over. There's a spot of blood on the end so I turn it round to use the other only there's a spot there too. I do the coke anyway before Nood notices. All I feel's paranoid tryin' to think of something to say.

— Go'a shit bad man..., I say dancin' around.

— Yeah?

— Kuf's laxed me up.

— Yeah...

We do another line why the fuck not. At least the sounds of drug-takin' break the silence an' cut out the need to talk. Then Marcello's squeezin' into the office out of breath haulin' up his trousers. Sweat's pourin' off of him glowin' in black rings round his eyes.

— I makea de special guest appearance, he announces with arms out toward the audience.

— Yeah a real honour scumpig, says Nood.

Marcello lurches forward so's Nood has to evacuate from the chair. Marcello slumps in his place grabbin' the rolled tenner for the last remainin' line. After it's up his nose he starts twitchin' an' laughin'.

— We fuck dose bastards good. Ay Nood-dell? Ay? Really good in de ass. Baba gonna cry like a girl.

— No he won't.

— Yes. And Iya Marcello Pinka Goose Molinari will be der to see it.

— No you fuckin' won't. Baba ain't gonna cry cos he ain't never gonna know shit. An' don't fuckin' forget it.

The words got no effect. Marcello's already pissin' himself. He slides off the chair onto his knees an' starts slappin' on the floor with garglin' noises comin' out his mouth.

— Baba gonna cry like a girl... Bab- gonn- cra- lickle-guh- he wi- cra-

— Shut the fuck up. Mar-Oi. Shut it.

— Thisa time we will be big and Mister Molinari will make a big stinky fart in de face of Baba and all his friends. One at a time. They gonna cry-

— SHUT THE FUCK UP.

— They gonna fucky cry because I-

— SHUT- THE- FUCK- UP, says Nood losin' it.

He grabs a hold of Marcello's shirt an' tries to pull him back onto the chair. The shirt's soaked up with sweat an' under it's a greasy pot belly. Nood sinks his hands into it.

— Shift ya fat italian cunt.

But Marcello's way too heavy an' don't wanna move anyhow. Nood lets go an' looks at me wonderin' what to do with him. But what's really goin' through his pissy coked up mind's how to make all the money for himself. Brain workin' overtime figurin' how to leave someone else to face the facts. An' Baba's one of the biggest facts around. But Nood ain't even doin' too good with the fat italian.

Marcello's sinkin' further an' further toward the floor laughin' hysterical. One of his shoes has come off.

— He gonna fucky cry like a lickle fucky giiirl... Ay Noo-Dell? Ay? I sheet in his mouth in de mouth of fucky girly Baba.

I hear Nood's teeth grindin'. He kicks the shoe into a corner then steps away from Marcello lookin' down at him like he's nothin'. Split second later he lifts his leg to stamp on him. I step in the way.

— Only make him worse man...

— Fuck off. Do him good bein' an insect...

Nood tries to hook his leg behind me aimin' stamps at Marcello's head.

— He's gonna blab his face off na mean. Get out the fuckin' road Tax. Can't get no worse.

— Can if you go'a explain all over how the geezer's head caved in by accident...

Nood backs off pushin' me away at the same time.

— You're just pussyin' out. Innit. Baba was righ' wasn't he. Eh?... You're pussy. You'll be lispin' an' reekin' of KY an' shit soon na mean.

His whole face is screwed up evil. I ain't never received that look. Ain't even me he's lookin' at. Just anythin' that's half way alive in front of him. Anythin' crawlin' that he can tread on.

— Fuck you, I say but there's nothin' behind it.

— Still righ' though wasn't he.

— Yeah. Like Big Chief Grinning Fool here was righ' about the deal: *It's so simple it's brilliant*. Innit Nood.

Nood goes for my throat teeth bared. I let him shove me backward against the wall. We seem to take forever to get there like we're floatin'. Everythin' slows. I take in the whole scene. Marcello's kinda still half on the floor half up makin' an effort but swayin' not movin' like he was hung off wires. Nood's seethin' through his teeth an' his lips move like he's about to say the final word. But nothin's comin' out. I see the face of Mary from Galway smilin' red blond meadow from a tape box. Shadows all over. There's a chant buildin' beyond the door.

Maybe the bare bulb swings. It's like there's moments when everythin' stops. Paused. An' you know you've missed a bit but it's too fucked up stupid to go back an' figure it all out.

— YOU THINK I'M PISSIN' ABOUT DON'T YA, Nood's screamin' in my face.

I let my arms hang.

— I just want my end out of this... Like now... Y'na mean I've had it... I've jus' had it man...

— *You've* had it... I don't give a fuck what you've had. I got responsibili'y now. I'm the one who says wha' goes na mean. I'm the one who's talkin' an' you're the one whass lissenin'. I don't need no fuckin' driver confrontatin' with me. I don't need no batty monkey on my fuckin' back. No pussy with no bottle talkin' at me. Cos I give the fuckin' orders. Cos I'm a fuckin' father. Thass righ' a *father*. A full on fuckin' daddy. Wha're you? A driver. A fuckin' driver is all. Whass tha'? It ain't nish. I'm a fuckin' father an' I do wha' I do. An' I do whass *right*.

— Yeah well lissen dad: I want my split... Sort us out. Now... Sort us out. I mean it. Jus' sort it man. Come on Nood do it... I've had i'.

Nood lets go of me an' his arm drops to his side. He backs off noddin' an' grindin' his teeth. Then he says real quiet:

— You wan' i'? You can have i'. You an' him both.

He pulls out the plastic bag then another rolled up wad from his balls. We ain't even discussed the split. I'm wonderin' how he's gonna position himself for the big negotiation. Which there always is. With a grand out this set up Nood could say three-way on a good day. Two hundred then a loada argument on a bad. He sparks a cig an' lets it burn in his mouth with his eyes screwed.

He counts out a ton. Then another. An' another like he's gonna count his whole freakin' fortune in front of me. Then he holds out four hundred.

— Four four an' a two for him.

He avoids lookin' at me. But it's when he actually passes the notes over countin' them out again into my hand that I realise I ain't gettin' out the Slice. An' with each crumpled up twenny goin' down on the one before I get more an' more sure of this. Whether he's spilled it to Kings an' Baba to save himself or knows about Koom an' Joey or all of this makes no difference. I'm fucked an' nothin'd make a difference. Nood can deal. He's a father. He does what's right. An' he can call in back-up. Specially today.

Marcello's wide awake now but still off his face not really computin' what's goin' down. He's comparin' his feet an' tryina figure why they look different. It's all turnin'. From the middle inside out. The chant in the hall's more a screamin' for blood.

— Well go on then. You're sorted. Fuck off back to the rave.

I put the money in a side pocket of my jacket so's Nood can see it even though he's makin' a show of ignorin' what I'm doin'. He's just stood there countin' an' shufflin' notes like he don't give a fuck.

— Alrigh', I mutter just to close the thing.

But it don't close shit. I kick Marcello's shoe toward him an' back out the office. Zeb's still on the decks mixin' scratchin' dancin' an' takin' shouts from the floor.

— MONSTER SOUND MONSTER SOUND OUND OUND...

The chantin's loud in my ear. There's a loada guys with their backs to me. All lookin' the same. Some laughin' yelpin'. I can't see beyond them but it's like the laughin's all at me. Shitsky turns round.

— Havin' fon bod? he says as I step up to him.

My fists're clenched by now. I blank him. Everythin's tight as I start to push through. An' I get that feelin' of bein' a ligger at someone else's do. The crowd kinda gives but don't open. Like they're all tryin' to stop me. I feel I'm gonna shit myself before I make it to the toilet.

Then I get through an' see what all the fussin's about. Stell Daise Steffi an' Char they're all limboin' in turns under a bar held up by Eamm an' Veej. They keep lowerin' it at the critical moment so's none of them ever make it collapsin' on the floor in fits. Then they scramble up goin' for it again each of them takin' shots of mescal on the way.

— NOOOD WHERE'S NOOD, Stell's screamin', HE'S GO'A WITNESS THIS...

Lendon passes me flashin' an urgent look. He leans in without breakin' his stride.

— Get your ass out front man. I'll wait for you. Do it.

Then he's gone. Baba's pullin' Char up off of the floor. She's totally soused eyes rollin'. He looks dead at me for a second. Then behind me toward the door of the office. I'm tryin' not to look back. Faces float by. The charlie's locked my mug into a dumb grin.

— Hey sheepkiller: where y'goin'? says Koom standin' in my way.

He's real leery with his short bruiser neck like a stump like mike tyson makes me wonder how or why I ever but it's too late now for that crap. I look him in the eye. Don't say nothin'. Fuck all to be said. Or done. Jumpin' out with Lendon's only gonna save what's comin' for a worse day. I walk around Koom to get to the toilet.

Push the door open an' hear it close behind. I think about which cubicle to use an' pick the middle one cos the catch is weak. No point gettin' them angrier tryina break down the door. My head's swimmin'. I flip the seat down with my foot undo my trousers pull them down takin' out the bag of Koom's money.

I sit down reachin' behind the toilet near where the pipe joins the wall an' stash it. Then I crap my guts out. Makes me exhausted. Slow. Like I could never move again. So I don't. Just wait sittin' there til the stench is like nothin'. Til all I hear's water tricklin' bubblin' in pipes basins plugholes.

Maybe they figure I just went in the toilet for my automatic. Maybe they figure I'm gonna come out guns blazin' or flingin' chinese death stars or all painted up with a knife in my teeth. That's funny. I wait. *Gary sucks cocks* it says on the side. Why's it always Gary? Like all across town there's a loada Garys blowin' their mates like they was born to do it. Want a blow phone Gary he'll sort ya. An' all Gary's mates're sittin' right now on toilets all across town writin' on toilet walls about the good times they had. Then I can smell the place again.

Seconds maybe minutes maybe more minutes later the main door opens. There's a loada footsteps. I lose it an' panic tryina wipe an' pull my trousers up but the door gets kicked in an' Baba blocks out the light. He grabs my tie pullin' me off the seat til I'm practically airborne. There's still spud caught in his teeth. Then my head's reelin' as he lands one on my face. A tooth's clinkin' around my mouth. I don't wanna swallow it. Or spit it out. I sort of hope it ain't a front one.

— Caught you with your pants down...

I hear Koom's laugh in the back.

— Never knew you felt that way 'bout me Bab, I mumble.

The tooth drops out.

— Fuckin' wiseass.

I look at him an' start laughin'. Can't exactly explain it. Next thing I let my head drop onto Baba's chest leavin' a bloodstain on his shirt. How many times he hits me after that I don't know. Maybe Koom gets his piece of me too. I think I hear him shoutin': *in the nose... in the nose.* Maybe the bare bulb swings. Maybe it's just Baba castin' shadows wide as houses. An' maybe none of this is happenin'. Lyin' on the cold shitty tiles I feel ribs clickin' crackin' as kicks connect. I'm makin' groanin' noises that I got no control of. Nood's voice.

— Shouldna gone self-employed y'cunt... Nobody does people what owes me cos I'm the only one wha' can do 'em yeah. Cunt... Stitched us all up Kings... Guy's fuckin' lawless na mean.

I rest my head on the floor. Nood's got his hand in my pocket repossessin' his dough. Then my keys. He knows I'll take it stumm. Like a man. Don't ever say you're innocent is all.

— Where's mine? Where the fuck's mine? says Koom.

I roll on my side cos the light's in my eyes. Tiniest spider I seen's hangin' off the back of the bowl. Wildlife. Really. I close my eyes to it. Like I could sleep through it. Baba prods into me with his foot.

— Oi. Scuzzhead. You listenin'? You listenin'? You got anything to say about Koom's money... Cos you know what choppin' is. OI I'M FUCKIN' TALKIN'...

So I turn my head in the direction of Baba's voice. Can't really see much.

— Got your attention have I? Not inconvenient to talk? Good... You know what choppin' is don't you?

I try to say yes but nothin' comes out. There's no air in me.

— WHERE'S MA FUCKIN' PAPERWORK? Koom shouts in my ear. Wastin' our fuckin' time Baba. Stamp 'im out. No: frisk him man. Frisk him down first then do it.

— Ain't friskin' him fathead he's covered in shit... Nothin' down his pants anyway.

— Gaaaa. Only good for schoolgirls innit. Innit. INNIT, says Koom layin' into my shins. So where's ma fuckin'-.

— Mine..., I mumble tastin' blood.

— Whass 'e say? He said som'in. Wha' d'ya say? Oi...

— Mine, I say louder.

— Yours? The fuck you say... Whass 'e sayin' Baba? Whass 'e mean?

— I'm sayin' it's at mine... Your dough... my place. Under the mattress...

Stupid to say the mattress. I wonder what the spider would say. Just hope they don't take me along to make sure.

— Be'er fuckin' be, says Koom. Let's take him in case it's a wind up.

— He'll fuck up the car. Bleedin' like a stuck pig, says Nood.

— Take *his* car. Stick him in the boot.

— Nah... forget him, says Baba still in my face. Cos he knows I'll come back an' chop him good. What you think Kings?

— He's punished. Leave him. Not like he's gonna run off. And there's no way I'm dragging him through the place. Besides I wanna get back and enjoy...

— Yeah righ', says Baba. He'da given the money back anyway.

— Y'na mean, Koom chimes.

They all have a laugh. Baba lifts me by my tie an' punches me in the side of the head one more time. For luck I guess. But I don't even feel it.

— Nobody fucks with me.

I dunno which one of us says that. Or maybe someone else says it. Or I just think it. Next thing I know I'm blubbin' like Nood's mum. Like a girl. Funny thing is it's for no reason I can think of. I could be laughin'.

— Look at him weepin'.

— Gaaaaaaaa.

They move off an' the door opens. Ravin' noise chatter music giggle. Closes behind them an' they're gone. The light's still bright in my face. I rest my head back on the floor. Take in air through my mouth but not enough.

Everythin's turned blurry warm numb. My eyes close. I suppose I'm tired. Or more tired. Or still tired. How long they'll be gone is the thing. They ain't exactly in a rush. I ain't exactly gonna skip home. The Slice might as well be maximum security. My body's Alcatraz with busted ribs for bars. An' I'm doin' life. Koom'll wait til the end. Drinkin' beer an' crackin' inside jokes. They all will. They'll all drift out together go to mine an' rip it up with Nood leadin' the way.

An' the whole time they'll be organisin' their money an' other people's money an' most other people's time. They'll be tryina squeeze that bitty extra out their dumb lives. That bit of magic that makes it all worthwhile. Fuck 'em. Assholes. Maybe. But who's dealin' what where's beyond workin' out. Things go blue in my head. Warm an' numb. I lose track. An' go to sleep.

Way past eleven

— It's way past eleven an' gone twelve so fock off, Joe's sayin' somewhere.

I open my eyes. They feel battered. The spider's connected a thread to my nose. I reach for the stash. Suddenly everythin's pain. Ribs pressin' in so's I can't breathe. The stash I'm tryina get into my sock only I can't bend enough to do it. Jam it in a pocket instead. I'm pullin' myself off of the floor as Joe come in. We open the door of the cubicle at the same time him lookin' at me an' me at the handwritten note taped to the door: *well out of order.*

— Well I t'ought I'd be hosin' down the lavvy tonight but this takes the cheese, says Joe scannin' the blood an' shit.

— Slipped off the seat didn't I. I'd help you mop up bu'- Joe grabs my arm to steady me.

— I s'pose you'll be wantin' some medical assistance...

— Nah, I say makin' toward the basins, I'd only have to join the special queue for friends of Nood.

I throw water on my face. Wash the blood out my achin' mouth. One of my smilin' teeth is missin'. I can hardly see out my left eye it's so swolled up. Could be worse. Nobody ever said I was pretty.

— There anyone out there?

— Mostly no.

— See Marcello?

— They all took off. At fockin' last. I mean I don't mind-

— Jus' gimme a hand to the door yeah.

— With pleasure...

I feel like I'm gonna heave. Joe feels it too an' half runs me through the main room. No sound except our steps. Nothin' left except the wreckage.

— Don't you fockin' dare...

He gets me to the exit nods goodnight an' starts shuttin'. I stick my foot in the way.

— Borrow us a tenner Joe.

— Fock off.

He slams it shut. Bolts it. I throw up right outside the door hopin' he fuckin' steps in it. I look up an' down the street in my puke-stained blooded up suit. I'm really there. All I need's a crumpled up can of spesh.

The street's long dead. The vehicles've all gone. The vans an' beemers an' four wheelers. They taken mine too. No way I'm walkin' streets in this state. I wrench off my tie an' forget it on the floor like I ain't gonna need it. The only thing I remember's a jack in a bin. So I pick it out. I was gonna use it for what? Now it's gonna be a car. I shuffle off just to get away from the Slice not knowin' where I'm headed. The Harrow Road's full of dogshit that comes alive after dark. An' there's no stone to crawl under.

So I turn in a sidestreet lookin' for a car that ain't too obvious. I find a well knocked out Renault 4 that I break into easy with the jack an' drive off into the cold metal night. Where I don't know. Just sittin' in the seat's killin' my ribs. They probably staked out my place so I can't show there.

I start countin' my friends. At least the people I could knock. Those that'd help me in the meantime before I can get back in. Cos if I don't get back in I could go anywhere. It don't matter. Blow it all out like I was a rebel. I could drive all night. If I had a Vespa I could ride it down to Brighton like an asshole with rock music in my ear an' my parka flyin' in the wind an' junk it in the sea like my old dreams was all broken an' the new dawn was just up the road. Instead I'm drivin' to Keef's.

Fifteen after twelve

Thrash it down Ladbroke Grove hard as I can. Under Westway. In an' out the light. Then left onto Westbourne Park. Powis Square Ledbury Chepstow Bishop's Bridge through to Bayswater round Paddington an' on to Marble Arch into the streamin' traffic. I squint at headlights. I take bends. I climb pavements. I bleed from my fuckin' face into the night. The joy of ridin'. Kills all pain for seconds at a time. The car's rackety. I turn on the radio:

...And this next one's the chart-busting debut single from Manchester-based band The Saddies...

So I flip to FM crossin' the West End where it gets brighter. Mercs dinner jackets middleage blondes straight from their hairdos. Dressed up drinkers swaggerin' with the change they licked out their boss's ass. Dazzled up buzz junkies filin' out shite fuckin' shows an' arcades. Walls of white neon. Arguin' couple at a traffic light:

— *I just can't believe you're being like this...*, he says.

— *And I can't believe you're being like this...*, she says.

South to Waterloo where the sun went down. Plenty of people strollin' the bridge peekin' over at the current an' readin' tomorrow's weather in the sky. Like it mattered. Or takin' snaps with flash. Like all they got is what they remember. I turn straight to the dead Elephant which ain't nothin' but a roundabout. There's a night bus stalled in a box junction. Walworth Road to Camberwell Green where it gets darker an' jumbled an' the dark itself sneaks in everywhere. There's static on the FM with pirates burstin' in an' tecno jungle garage hip hop blarin' out:

...Big Mal says nuff respect to the firin' posse down six oh nine... Droppin' this one for the people...

An' into Peckham. Cabs yardies cops. Barred offies. A yellow jeep with *Black Ash* sprayed on the side. Late night store with lumpy guys in puff jackets on a munchy hunt. Vandals in a sidestreet who ain't gettin' up for school. Peckham's most people's nightmare. But least it ain't Kilburn. An' the purple hole in my smile'll ward off evil.

Keef's is one of these yellow neon streets that looks like a million others. Everythin' blurred to the same level of yellow dark from sky to pavement like a paper bag over my head. I park up ease out the car hopin' to keep my back straight. Every step jars my bones. An' with the pain again I can't remember what it was like without.

I get myself up the steps an' knuckle the front window. Through the curtain there's blue electric flashes of tv. After a second Keef peers out from a crack presses his face against the glass hands cupped over his eyes. Don't look like he recognise me. Or don't wanna. Then he shows at the creaky door in Y-fronts his mug raw red an' skin flabby white scratchin' his eyebrow.

— Fuckin' 'ell Tax... Fuck happen to you?

I try not to look at him. Cold sweat on my back. Glance behind down the street instead which only give Keef the fear. He steps back so's the front door covers half his face.

— Whass goin' on? Whass-

— Listen... Need a place to crash. For a coupla nights...

— Yeah?

This ain't Keef's number one choice for the evenin' but he ain't gonna refuse. He can't.

— ...Well yeah sure. Course. No sweat no fuckin' sweat..., he says steppin' aside, I mean anytime anyfuckin' time Tax you know tha'... Well... Come in then...

I step in an' he shuts the door. Suddenly we're standin' too close to each other in the corridor. He dunno where the fuck to put himself so he edges by.

— Well steamy nigh' innit..., he says pullin' up his pants.

I half nod an' follow after him along a sticky lino passage to his gaff. Then down another passageway to the kitchen which is yellower than the street. The table's loaded with empty cans an' grease an' a half-eaten Golden Temple takeaway. For some reason I make sure there's no scum on the chair before I sit.

— Wanna beer? says Keef openin' the fridge an' pullin' a can.

— Cup tea...

We dunno what to say so we keep ourselves busy. Keef pours some lager down his throat to get in the mood. He sprays water into the kettle an' dumps it on the cooker scratchin' his ass then his eyebrow. I search my pockets for my piece of leb. He burps a big one an' looks over like I'm supposed to say *nice one*. I take out matches.

Keef grabs a binliner shovellin' whatever's on the table into it. Only it's ripped where it counts. Sweet an' sour or whatever leaks out. He drops the whole thing on the floor an kicks it in a corner.

My nose keeps dribblin'. I wipe it on my sleeve when Keef's not lookin'. Like I got appearances to keep up. Keef flips some skins on the table. I start billin' one up with him watchin' out the corner of his eye. A piece of screwed up plastic's expandin' out in the bin. An' the fridge is clackin' out some dance beat that any DJ would kill for. It all means somethin' when you ain't got horseburger to say. But Keef don't hear nothin'. 'Ventually he's gettin' very nervy waitin' for the kettle to boil or me to break the silence.

— Oi Tax: you wanna get som'in for them cuts. Go septic on ya uvverwise...

I don't say nothin'. Just carry on crumblin' in the hot hash.

— Got some stuff. I'll get i', says Keef after a moment.

He pads off somewhere an' brings back a shoebox of pills an' medicine an' leaky mixture which he sticks in front of me. One particular bottle containin' red lotion cak he opens under my nose like the smell's gonna convince me it works.

— This gear's the business... I should know...

The kettle starts to rattle on the cooker. Keef's waitin' for a verdict on his wonder lotion but I keep my head down. He leaves the gear on the table an' sorts the tea. With his back turned I spark the spliff. The first pull fills my head. Then moves down my whole body. I slump wantin' a bed.

— How do you take it? says Keef over his shoulder.

— In the shitter, I mumble.

— Ain't funny Tax... Wha' 'bout your tea?

— Three sugars. Milk.

Keef puts the tea down in front an' sits opposite with this cheesy *well here we are* grin. I stir a long while.

— Left the bag in..., says Keef like someone's mum.

He's really tryin'. I can feel he's itchin' to hear the details. But I just stir slow thinkin' it was a big mistake turnin' up.

— Whass the story then Tax...

— Shoulda seen the lamppost Keef...

— Serious man...

Sounds weird Keef sayin' *man* to me. Like he's tryina sound back in with half of North London. Some people just shouldn't say it. It's like me sayin' *left the bag in*. I stand leavin' the spliff smokin' on the edge of the table an' head for the toilet. As I pass Keef's bedroom a ranky kinda reek hits me. I glance in an' see a wad of tissue by the bed.

Probably in the shape of his cock. I go piss tryin' not to breathe. There's a tacked up pullout of a sunny smilin' football team on the wall. Then I go back an' sit down hookin' my arms this way an' that tryina find comfort on the wooden chair.

Biscuits've appeared on the table. Half a packet. Lemon curd. I toke up the spliff. Keef probably thinks I'm windin' him up. Like I owe him laughs for floorspace.

— You gonna tell us then or wha'?

— Yeah Keef yeah...

— In your own time mate, he has to say with another cheesy grin.

After a couple more tokes I pass him the spliff not that it's gonna make a difference in his case.

— In a nutshell... I teefed Koom's money. An' as Koom'd say: I got hided.

— Wha' by Koom?

— Baba mostly. They're out lookin' for me. Baba an' everyone an' if they knew I's here they be after *you* for free.

— Me? What they want with me? I made my peace with 'em didn't I. I was square. Well square.

— Tough titty mate. I jus' declared war again for you.

— Why? Wha' for? What they still after you for? I mean if they done ya they done ya. Whass their problem? Thass the way it goes innit. It's socie'y. You paid the P.

— But I ain't paid 'em back.

— Yeah: well that's a point for you. That's your tough titty an' only yours. I cleaned *my* fuckin' slate.

— You go'a be jokin'. You never clean it. You jus' keep cleanin' it is all. Didn't anyone ever tell you: thass socie'y.

Keef goes quiet an' starts on his eyebrow again.

— Still... you'll be alrigh' innit Keef...

Keef twigs straight away an' doesn't look up.

— Yeah yeah I hope so, he mumbles.

— You'll be well cosy.

Keef pulls on his lager picks at some crust stickin' to the table then glances about. I just keep lookin' at him til he catches my good eye.

— Na mean, I say.

Why I have to carry on I don't know. I could just as easy shut the fuck up. Leave it at that. Let it go. An' then what.

— I'm gonna be cosy? Whassa' supposed to mean?

I take a sip of the tea. Weak old tea bag.

— Tax. Oi... Wha' the bollocks you tellin' me? Wha' d'y'mean I'll be-

— I mean you'd crawl up anyone's shit-stinkin' ass. Long as it's a bit warm an' crappy innit. Jus' to be in somewhere. Anyfuckinwhere. Don't matter to you does it... So that's what I'm sayin': you'll be cosy.

Keef's a bit gutted. He puts his tin down his red face gettin' redder mainly cos he don't know whether to shout lean in whisper threats stand up or jus' go for it an' start the slapstick. But he has to do somethin'.

— You crossed the fuckin' river to tell me tha'. Why don't you fuck off back to Kilburn. Go on, he says half standin' up over me, FUCK OFF BACK...

I look up at him an' smile even though it hurts my mouth. It really works. He kinda shrinks from that purple hole.

— ...If all you're gonna do is stir it...

Keef's voice fades leavin' it down to me to make peace with him. Then I suppose I can make my peace with *them*. An' it's all back to square one. Cosy. I get up. *They ain't never gonna take me alive*. As they say.

— I'm goin'...

But I sort of lag instead. Long enough for even a dummy like Keef to *fink*. As deep as he can.

— Where y'gonna go? Go on 'en where? You're puffed up nothin'. You're nothin' y'cunt. Not withou' Nood an' the rest of 'em. Not without back-up... Where y'gonna go? Jus' walk out on your mates your posse you're nothin'. Wha' you gonna do? Go on the piss on y'tod innit. Keel out in a fuckin' gutter innit. Or you'll be out wipin' off car windows. Fuckin' Ragboy. Or workin' down mcdonalds innit. Like a cunt. Or divin' through people's windows with a shiv an' a gee o' ramraider up y'nose. You need to sort yourself out an' all y'cunt. Get a trade. Get a fuckin' trade. They learn me that inside. The fuckin' hard way. Your trade's your lifeline. *Never too late to go straight*. Thass wha' they say innit. I take my fuckin' thick ear an' I bounce righ' back. Thass righ'. Blue in the fuckin' face I don't care. I know where I fuckin' stand... I...

So I look down to where I'm standin'. There's lino coverin' the floor with a loada green spirals on red squares. I fell into lino like that the first time I took acid round my friend's house. We was mickey mouse faceless travellin' through space. Then we arrived at this monster planet which was his mum. Suddenly I was dancin' round the kitchen with her. She got right into it shakin' her hams about. She kept askin' why we was so happy. We told her we'd passed an exam. She broke out some sweet brandy. We all got pissed. We was laughin' mad with tears rollin'. Jiggin' a red square mambo wha'ever. Twelve hours later I was still laughin' with lipstick blotchin' up my face. Then I came back down.

Keef's still talkin' me through his rehab programme.

— ...You don't know shit. You go'a climb the ladder one step at a time. You don't even fuckin' know which way's up. You'll be back. Thass righ'. You will. You will I know tha'. One way or the other...

— Oh yeah? I say movin' toward the door.

— Yeah cos what you gonna do?

— Ain't gonna eat shit sandwich thass for sure.

— You wanna try eatin' shit sandwich some time. Makes eatin' humble pie a lot easier.

— Nice: that come to you in a dream did it. Or did someone learn i' you the *hard way*?

Keef takes a step toward me an' just sneers evil in my face.

— You'll be back... An' it won't be like no Arnold Schwarzafucka.

I wanna bust his dumb fuckin' mug wide open an' watch all the dumbness spillin' out. But for now all I can do is swallow then turn an' walk out along the sticky lino passage an' slam the creaky front door. The street's still yellow. I expected a fuckin' rainbow. An' the tv's still flashin'. I imagine Keef starin' at it can in one hand scratchin' an eyebrow with the other. Bidin' his time til the Nummas forgive an' forget. Or Baba discovers he's really a woman. Whichever come first. Cos Keef's livin' his fuckin' life like there was nothin' else. Just livin' it. Beer bogroll bed.

Somewhere further north there's Lendon with his beemers an' bitches. Bangin' with the rudeboys. Now armed an' dangerous. Down with the massive. Way out in space. An' the rest are just playin' follow my leader round the north west zone. I have to square things with Char. What I have to prove to her I don't know. Som'ing. Only there's nothin' 'cept a sewer connectin' Peckham an' Stonebridge.

One eleven

The Renault won't start like it's committed suicide on me. After turnin' it over a few times a light comes on in a first floor window. A second later the light goes off leavin' a moon face starin' out. So I wait til it disappears. Can't risk tryin' to start it again an' new wheels is out the question. Peckham's heavin' with the wrong people. I get out an' walk to the high street headin' for the first cab office.

Further up the street by the main junction there's an empty police van back doors open an' a bit of activity that I can't really see. But some girl's wailin' bad:

— JAAY. RUUUN. JUST RUUUN. HE'S GOT A KNIFE. WHY DOESN'T HE RUN? WHY DOESN'T HE RUN? WHY DOESN'T HE RUN?

I walk the other way stickin' to the dark. Up ahead the wire security door of *Ryda Cars* is half closed. A ball of weed smoke sits on the pavement concealin' a half dozen fuckers inside slouched out mashed on armchairs an' boxes. I lean in tryina hide my swollen face from the bare light.

— Yeah? says the one nearest clockin' me cockeyed from under a slopin' hat.

— How much to Stonebridge?

He looks round at the others in turn with this hummin' laugh. An' the others all pitch in til they're all hummin' an' slappin' their knees.

— Stonebridge? I hear Stonebridge? Man you're talkin' a mortgage. Get me? Ain't nobody goin' to Stonebridge tonight.

— Jus' gi's a price.

— Thir'y pound. Up front, says a fat white phantom hand with a gold ring that just appears from the control box behind the counter.

— You go'a be jokin'.

— You heard the man. Take it or leave it. Stonebridge even the milkman's on dangermoney y'get me.

— Mugged f'y'pizzarup'er'innit, says a raggy moustache with a spliff.

They look round at each other noddin' slow an' blowin' through their noses like weird fish.

— You still 'ere?

— Yeah as it goes... Alrigh'... fifteen now... an' fifteen on delivery...

— Jesus fuckin' christ who's the cunt? says Hand wavin'. Ge'm the *fuck aaht*.

Slopey Cockeye puts his hands on the sides of his chair an' makes like he's gonna stand. I blow out my nose at him an' start to back out still actin' tough when there's a big jumble from the back of the place an' someone clappin'.

Through the smoke comes Fola shirt open to his navel. He's still doin' up his flies laughin' actin' drunk with his shoulders hunched an' the collar of his black leather jacket pointin' straigh' up at the ceilin'. Like his whole day's just been one big kickback before the comin' of night.

— HEY GROOVAH: that was tha most *to-tahly* smashing piss I evah have.

— Hey Fola how y'doin'? I say steppin' in to shake.

— Well a'right man, he says slappin' my ribs, to-tahly groovy babesville yeah. You look like-

— Wanna go Stonebridge tonigh'?

— He don't give up do he, says Raggytache.

— Nigeria's answer to Gary Glitter'll sor' Mr. Stonebridge, says Hand sour.

— Gary Glittah boosh, says Fola spinnin' on his heel. I am John Shaft: *sex machine to all tha chicks SHHHHAAAFT... damn right...*

— 'Ooever the fuck you is tonigh' Folashit, says Hand, the question is is you is or is you ain't goin' dahn Stonebridge—

— I go anywhere anytime like diss, says Fola clickin' his fingers. Folafreedomsoulbrothamothah take you to Stonebridge like nothing. I take you to HEV-ON with the powah of my naturahl high yeah. What is happening in Stonebridge? Killah babes? Slip and slide? Supahfly? Fly by night? Lov Box Monday Speshahl? *To-tahly* smashing.

— In y'dreams, says Slopey Cockeye.

— Do not listen to this sad fornicatoh. He knows nothing about tha pahtee spirit. I am an agent of god.

— Wha' in an S reg cortina?

So we step outside leavin' the crew all noddin' an' blowin' out their noses. I ease into the furlined front of Fola's Cortina complete with furry dice danglin' off of the mirror an' waggin' dog in the back. Cheap gadgets glow green from the dash or from some weird hang. The wheel's coiled with red chilli lights. Fola guns it all up til it screams an' we jump out in the road.

— You look like a big boiled turkey ass man, he says tappin' the speedo.

Fola's clock says eight twenty

We head toward Vauxhall pickin' up speed all the time with Fola breakin' reds an' slicin' traffic like the rules of survival didn't apply. He keeps glancin' at me. Which I ain't gonna hold against him.

— What happen? No wait. Upon reflection nevah mind don't tell me I don't want no tale of sorrow to mess my groove.

— Nothin's gonna do tha' man. How come you didn't show at Nood's?

— The wedding? You ah cray-zee. It would not suit my image on the dancefloor to be looking like you ah... I mean how ah you going to score looking like that?

— I'll get sympathy.

— You will get arrested. Bot you know Nood and them these ah not friends of mine they ah gangstah peepull. Bot I am not no gangstah. You know?

— Yeah yeah...

— *Seri-ass* shit man. I flah my kite and that is that. Gangstah peepull they have to earn their bones all tha time. You know. That is nevah my thing. I prefah *laid back activity*. Bottah on toast. You hear me?

— I hear ya, I say reachin' down an' flippin' on the radio.

...and I'll be hosting RAVE WICKED with special guest Miss Plush of the Year showing off the baddest gear live and direct from the Motherland...

But Fola don't take the hint.

— I got my scammin' ways dass tha name of tha game. How else you can *pahtee* I mean really *pahtee*. You must feathah your bed in *advance* and take care of numbah one sure. But Nood and tha crazy gang ah not real smashing people. You hear me right because you like to *pahtee*. I seen you *pahtee* man. Wicked akshon groovah tequila coke billion dollah babe pull up to my bompah ok dass tha name of it boss. Bot nothing comes out from nothing. I mean to say all tha politicians steal any money they can with their computah and there is no piece of cake left except tha crombs. Then gangstah people steal tha *crombs*. I mean like now with a face like yours you should be applying for *disability allowance*. No joke. Give me a half a chance I would be op for dat like *diss* and it would not be a crime because it is jost like dipping my fried chickon into tha *sauce*. Give me spice for life. You know what I mean.

— Sure I do...

I nod an' mumble starin' out. Slide down in the seat kinda passin' out too. Spinnin' not rinsin' with the whole of it goin' by. A busted traffic light. A dented streetlight. A stream of brick wall with grafitti: *Lord Have Mercy*. But it don't look like he did cos behind the wall's already rubble. Fola swerves to avoid a hole in the road steerin' with a finger always about to die in fourth like he can't shift down.

— I'm talkin' *sauce*. A'right. Like last night I have two babes in the back from a big flash clob in tha west end. They wah both of them loaded and rolling in tha back so I could see everything I mean *everything*. Sweet juice of tha melon fruit. One of them wah wearing nothing undah and I sweh I could see wetness down there. *To-tahly* smashing like a pahtee invitayshon. I jost could not concentrate on my *driving*. You know what I am saying. Impulses ah leading me into temptation. After a while I can stand no more. So ahround Cambahwell I stop tha car and say look: you ah two drop dead babes and you ah locky because I am John Shaft. They look at each othah and start to freak man like someone attack them in their *own* home. They try to get out. Bot of course I fix tha doors so you have to open from outside. By tha time I'm out to let *them* out they ah screaming blue murdah. I open tha door and they jost try to ron bot not before Folasoulbrothah get a handful of *pussy*. You know: jost to check if it is really *wet*.

Fola looks at me grinnin' gold.

— So what do you think: wet or dry?

— Drippin'. Like melted cheese under your blowtorch eyes.

Fola busts his gut slappin' the wheel an' lookin' at me laughin' his head off til I have to remind him of the unfoldin' road situation.

— You kill me man. Wicked. A'right. That is *to-tahly* exact: they wah hot to trot but could not handle numbah one grooveridah.

Fola cuts up whatever traffic's left round Marble Arch an' gets onto Edgware Road still slappin' the wheel.

— Wicked... blowtorch eyes... smashing...

Late night falafel temples turn to dark blocks on Maida Vale then to juiceheads hangin' out by the State on Kilburn High. Feels like I been on holiday.

— So where ah you going?

— Mine then Stonebridge. Jus' carry on...

— Why Stonebridge? Who is in Stonebridge? Your American Girl? Your sympathy babe? She will rock and roll you in ha ahms like-

— Zip it man.

— I can tell that you ah not relaxing. You can tell Folafreedom any type of problem because Folafreedom been and lived it already.

— I go'a see someone.

— *A woo-man?*

— Yeh...

— What kind of high-class chick live in Stonebridge? Or ah you looking for low-class akshon? Because you know-

— I jus' go'a make my peace with someone.

— Ohhhhh... big gangstahstyle...

— No man... no, I say wasted. Just a friend...

— Jost a friend boosh. You have *lov* tenshon. You know? You ah in *lov*.

— Fuck you talkin' about?

— Take my advice and wait for intahflorah in tha morning. What kind of high-class akshon is going to look you up and down and place their lips upon yours ansah me that.

— Well it's now or never sor'a thing...

— Ooooh ok wildwest style.

— Just do a righ' at the next light. Under the viaduct...

We turn onto Maygrove. I sink in the seat far as I can scannin' all over. Fola watches me nervous.

— Big trouble I can tell. What ah you going to do?

— Turn it round an' jus' drive past one more time.

The lights in mine are on an' the curtains drawn but it all seems quiet. I coulda left it like that myself. I don't remember. I look round for any cars I know searchin' the plates for letters I recognise. But it's easy to miss somethin'. No smashed windows nothin'. Even if they been here it's difficult to believe they're still inside ready to rush me. They woulda trashed the place real quick. Grabbed my stuff when they couldn't find no money for Koom. Then dumped my car. Or trashed it too. They woulda just been an' gone swearin' to come again an' rip my liver out.

But then again they could be up there. Playin' poker for matchsticks. Eatin' pizza. Few licks of vodka. An' workin' their way through a neat pile of kuf wraps. Keepin' themself simmerin' the whole time. Ready to boil an' really fuckin' charge. I ain't takin' that chance. I tap Fola.

— Ok less go Stonebridge... North of Hillside yeah?

Fola shrugs happy to move out. We head across the junction onto Christchurch then right onto Willesden Lane droppin' down to Harlesden an' Craven Park. Stonebridge is to the west with the North Circ cuttin' off the escape route on one side. The river is on the other side with Brent junction an' a mass of railway to the south. Like divin' in a cage. Control bust in on the airwave:

Fola come in this is Ryda control where is you I got jobs stackin' up all over it's a busy circuit... a busy circuit...

The broke up streets made sleek in the nightlight give nothin' away. Nothin' about anythin' that happens or could happen. Everywhere there's bolted doors basements an' a loada people driftin' always after a hit a party always knockin' ringin' listenin' out for signs of life. Or sleekin' through the night alone just lookin'.

The estate creeps up. One minute it's streets you could find in a square on a map. Then it's there. You're in it but you never know if it's the middle or the edge. The only maps're in your head. It's impossible to know it less you live it. Everythin' looks sly to the people that don't. Every walkway face flower lone dog on a leash draggin' a shadow. Every shout moan laugh cough scrapin' squeakin' of shoes. Char did say to come round. Fola pulls up.

— *Broken glass everywhere,* he sings from Grandmaster Flash. I am not going no furthah.

— Safe... Listen you up for stickin' around twenny minutes. Make it worth your while...

Fola raises his eyebrows.

— My while is worth more than rice and peas my-

I snap him fifty from my roll.

— Ok bigspendah style. So what ah you going to do in twenty minutes not fifteen not twenty five? Hah? You plan to make a play for ha? You figure twenty minutes succeed or fail. Eithah way you ah out of there like curry from a skinhead's mouth. Right?

— Som'in like that yeah. You in?

— Fifty talk... Bot a word of advice from Folafreedom on your *overall approach*: You bettah try to look smoothah for success. You most behave like a true champion, he says clenchin' up both fists, *Po-si-ti-ve* thinking. *Coal-mine* attitude. Be *pro-jecting* yoh image all tha time.

I start to get out.

— Thass fifty quid's worth of advice? Thanks I'll keep it in mind.

— No wait, says Fola gettin' out after me.

He goes round the back an' opens the boot takin' out some silver garm like it was Saturday night at Stallions.

— *Silvah killah bombah jacket*: dress to impress, says Fola pullin' off my jacket with one hand. Billiondollah style...

— I'm gonna look dumb...

— Trust me joyridah. You will not look more dumb.

It makes some kind of sense. I shake Silver Killer on my shoulders. Low profile it ain't. Fola slaps my back grinnin'. I grin back with pain.

— A'right. Smashing. Ease that lov tenshon. Shoot yoh shots cowboy. I will wait here...

Dead on two

I walk across a patch of grass watchin' for dog cak then between two blocks to a stairwell. Charmaine's on the second. The stairs're crisp with glass. Hers is right at the end of a corridor of flats with frosted safety glass double locks even some bars. I flip the letter box twice an' look out over the balcony. I can see half Fola's car. He's chattin' to control. Nothin's happenin' behind so I flip the box again only louder. Char comes to the door an' opens it on the chain smilin' for a second til she sees it's me.

— Hi Charmaine..., I say uneasy.

— God almighty wha'ppen?

She's still bleary an' pissed an' beautiful an' just stands there slouchy with a towel round her withou' openin' the door.

— Go'a talk... Can we talk?... Inside...

— Well... I'm... It's late Tax. I have to get up man. Y'na mean... Wha' happen to you?

— I just go'a talk a bit... serious... do I look like I'm on a date?

— Nice jacket...

— Come on Char... please...

— I would bu' thing is... there's someone s'posed to be comin'... Like any minute. I'm jus' waitin' up...

— Who? I'll be gone... Come on...

Char caves in straightens up shuts the door to unhook
the chain then opens it with a smile. I go in. Smells of
laundry dryin' on a radiator. Hot dry. Late night tv goin'
somewhere in the back.

— It's really got be two minutes guy...

We go in the kitchen an' suddenly can't look at each
other in the hard striplight. Or more like I can't look at her.

— I'd make tea bu'-

— Iss ok...

— You want som'in' else?

— Nah no iss ok really...

She waits for me to start talkin' but it's just a mess in my
head. I'm tryina figure the right order of words. I'm even
tryina think what Fola would come up with. Some crazy
fuckin' line an' it would all end with tequila an' Char
callin' in sick in the mornin'. *Boosh.* I start a cigarette that
I don't really want.

— Look... I...

The whole audience is laughin' on the tv.

— ...I sor'a got into some trouble. But it ain't the way
they're gonna tell it... Koom... You know Koom? An' Joey?
His brother. The two-

— I heard somethin' yeh. People was talkin'... I was a
bit... Some BNP people go'm right? Bastards man. So what
'bout it?

— It was me.

— You...

I sort of blink at her.

— You're sayin' it was you what?

— I did it... Nazis... tha' was all... separate... 'nother
story...

— You beat them up? Koom an' whassisface? You?

I give one little nod like it was a little thing. She stares
at me. Maybe she expects a big nod an' a bow. It's
impossible to know what she thinks.

— You?

I don't move an eyebrow in case it's the wrong eyebrow.
— You?
— Yeah that's what I said I did it me. What d'y'want a fuckin' diagram.

Char takes a breath takes the pack of cigarettes out my hand takes a seat at the table an' sparks one. She holds the match out in front of her eyes an' lets it burn black just fixed on it. Real fuckin' dramatic.

— Can't believe it. I- Why? Why d'y'do it? she says raisin' her voice.

Wha'm I gonna say? I mean the usual answer to the question *why* is *fuck you*. But like I've already pushed it far enough.

— Tax: I'm askin' you: Why the fuck d'you do it?

If she didn't ask maybe I'd say all kindsa things right out of my head. But I know exactly what typea answer she's expectin'. So I give it.

— They had the goods innit.
— Oh boy..., she practically groans.

She puts the cigarette into an ashtray an' smoothes down the sides of her hair with both hands. She's lookin' at nothin' an' shakin' her head real heavy an' pastin' on the gloom like she don't get the chance often enough. Too tired to scream me out. She just makes a show of blankin' me instead concentratin' on stretchin' a loose hair from her forehead. After it's stretched tight she coils it round a finger an' jerks it out.

— You know... one day you should take five an' listen to yourself... *they had the goods innit*, she says wide-eye an' slow like I was a moron. I mean don't you *give* a fuck-

— *Me* give a fuck? Who you waitin' for then: a mobile phone salesman in a range rover with all round stereo. An' tinted windows for those magic moments on the hard shoulder of the M25. Fuck...

— I don't have to listen to this, she says standin' not knowin' whether to fold her arms.

She picks up the cig for somethin' to do.

— Shit... Char-

— You should go.

I look down at the floor an' feel her lookin'. I still ain't said what I came to say. Wha'ever it was.

— ...I'm... sorry...

She looks at me with this *oh yeah sell me double glazin'* expression on her face.

— I was mashed Char. Wha' can I tell you. I never was like that. You know I wasn't. You said so yourself. Didn't you. You said that. I don't know wha' happened. I jus' did it. Thass all. I fucked up.

— Big time.

— So it was big time. I know tha'. An' maybe it's for the better. Who knows? Who does know? People change innit. Some of them. Iss better to think some things through innit. Then make a choice na mean. Iss done now. Things is wha' they is. Wha'm tryin'- It... I you know... I wouldn't do it again.

— Tha' come with a five year guarantee does it?

— Wha' can I say? I'm sorry 'bou' i' now. Thass all I came to tell you. Cos they're gonna tell you things. Wha'ever they say it ain't the way it happened. I ain't goin' back in with 'em. No way. I just ain't. No way.

— Yeah the karate kid goes straight don't tell me.

— You don't get it do you. I'm tryina tell you... som'in'. Maybe I fucked up big. Bu' iss a big thing I'm tellin' you now. You never get them out your head. Nobody does.

— Who?

— Who... *Them* ... The fuck- All of 'em. Iss a life thing na mean. Even now... Even now. I know I got a big mouth sometime an' I talk a loada cak bu' what's it mean?... Don't mean nothin'. Never did. An' I know it never did now...

— Yeh... righ'... I'm supposed to understand all tha'. The bullshit's better cooked on a meat feast pizza na mean. An' it looks better too...

Heavy. But when she sees my gutted face hers changes too.

— Hey Tax... I'm sorry righ' I didn't mean-

— Fuck...

I look at Char feelin' wacked. Kinda gutted. Expected somethin' else. Still expectin' somethin'. But she ain't even up for understandin' nothin'.

— Look... maybe you should go now Tax. We'll talk properly na mean. When you're makin' more sense. I mean it... An' I'm sorry abou' sayin' wha' I said... Bu' I ain't standin' round takin' this righ' now... Ok?

— Sure it's ok wha' the fuck.

I shrug a big empty shrug. It's like there's nothin' left to say an' she ain't said nothin'. Or maybe she's said everythin' but in a different language. Like two people with different headphones on dancin' past each other. She starts movin' toward the kitchen door. Passes me like furniture. Blanks me the whole time. So I follow tryina exchange a look.

— We'll talk yeah?

— Yeh yeh def...

— We'll talk...

— Yeh... I said...

We move to the front door just two shapes in a corridor. Anyone anywhere. An' that's it. Fuck can I say. I open an' step out. The air's cool. I flip my cigarette over the balcony. An' the first thing I'm aware of is the back of Baba's head disappearin' toward the stairwell. My gut just blows with adrenalin.

— Baba... Don't fuckin' believe it, I mumble.

— Yeah. I said...

— You didn't say it was him. I mean I saw you an' him- Charmaine these're his fuckin' dabs all over my face.

I must even look like a moron with my jaw hangin' loose. I grab hold of Char's arm to let her know it's no joke. But she's numb to the whole thing. Glass crackles on the stairs.

— I go'a hide somewhere, I'm whisperin', *now*...

— Hide? Hide where?

— Anyfreakin'where.

— Jesus... I don't- I can't believe you're gettin' me into this. I-

— Where?

Char just points without turnin' way down to the back past the livin' room. I'm movin' slicksnot into shadow.

— Bathroom... Airing cupboard... I don't believe this... I jus' can't fuckin'...

I get to the bathroom hearin' Baba's greetin' out front. I can't decide whether to shut the door or leave it half open. In the end I shut it leavin' a puddle of light at the bottom. Then I get in the airin' cupboard like it was nothin' an' shut that behind me too. The noise of the whole world's cut. Whatever's left of it's just burblin' strangled in metal pipes.

'Ventually I see edges. All the edges that surround me. The place is steamin'. There's a padded tank behind too hot to lean against so I have to squat on the floor with my knees to my chest. I'm sweatin' bathloads in the jacket so I slip it off. Char's panties're hangin' off a rail above my head. All different sizes like she was three people. There's a bathrobe on a peg. I lean toward it an' wipe my face. I think of her in her towel. An' Baba stickin' his hand under the tuck half way up her chest. I'm ashamed of the crap I talked. Like an asshole. A tap drips. So I find myself imaginin' if it's the bath or the sink an' what the fuck difference it makes. Only thing is I have to listen to it. Somethin' that's almost silence.

Air bubbles move round the cupboard carryin' a word or a noise from outside. I imagine their talk. I wanna hear them. Like I wanted to hear the voices in the drizzle that day but couldn't. Couldn't even hear the drizzle. Or the feet of the ant on Cee's leg. Or the sound it made when she trapped its back legs lettin' it struggle a while before smearin' it. Then she cleaned it off with spit on her finger. She looked at me embarrassed. I dunno if it was for killin' the ant or for cleanin' the mess. An' did mum smoke to ease the pain or for a sor'a joy that only she knew. Did anyone give a shit about a dead an' buried bastard. He never made no sound. Nor will I.

I remember my smokes on the kitchen table. A whole night cooped without a cigarette. Listenin' to the drips an' bubbles an' halfwords. Even if I wanna hear them talkin' I'd have to be in the main bit of the bathroom. But I can't do nothin' til Baba's had his piss. If I knew exactly where he was I'd have a chance of runnin' past him an' out. Leave Char to do the explainin'. Or maybe I could take him. But you can never hit a guy like Baba hard enough. If he's lyin' or bendin' down or with his back to me there's a good chance. I could punch his lights out. Rush him. Muller him. Kick his fuckin' head in. Rip his face off. Do him. Stamp him out.

I can't help lookin' round for a weapon but there's nothin' useful. An' even if there was I don't know if I could do it. Not after the three course cak I served up to Char. An' what if she looked me in the eye just before I wacked him. It's that hesitation that keeps me an' them separate. I never know if what I'm doin's the right thing. I can't know that. Nobody can. I didn't know it when I did Koom. I knew what I was doin' but that ain't the same. Even if they had it comin' it ain't necessarily right.

Them they always know. Baba always knows. Nood always knows. Lendon always knows. Right down to big local heros like Shabs an' Snipper. They all know. An' the rest go along like they knew. Like they'd never hesitate for a second. Like the decision's made.

One way or another I'm gettin' out of here. Least Fola ain't gonna take off in a hurry. Not with his jacket invested in my success. My legs're numb so I'm stretchin' them one at a time when there's a laugh. Char's laugh. A giggly kinda *fucked stoopid* laugh. She's doin' a great impression of someone havin' a really good time. Then the door of the bathroom's open. The cupboard lights up round me. Baba's bare feet slap across the lino in time to his short cracklin' breaths. Only a shitty door separates us. The loo seat's flipped. He pisses in the bowl. Then gobs in it. I wait for the flush but a tap's turned instead. He washes his hands. His knuckles probably sting under the cold water. Maybe he likes that feelin'.

Then silence again like the fuck's examinin' his ugly fuckin' mug in the mirror. Then there's a choppin' sound that I know's comin' from the top of the toilet. Metal on enamel. Baba's chalkin' a line in secret. He snorts an' slaps out again leavin' the door wide an' the toilet heavin'. An' leavin' me the whole night without a smoke.

I stand an' push open the cupboard door. The ball bearing spins. I wait a second then step onto the lino listenin' for voices. One of them puts a glass onto a glass table. They're in the livin' room just outside.

— It's like we been playin' cat an' mouse all this time, Baba's sayin', like I know you wanted me but somehow you always slipped through the net. Even when you was with Harris I knew you was still lookin'. Innit... Go on you have to say I'm right. You have to admit that right? I mean Harris was nothin' but a *pum pum* bandit. No no don't cos I know wha' you're gonna say. An' I know I shouldn't be dissin' him ok but this is about you an' me now. An' I just know in my heart you was lookin' the whole time innit. I *know* the signs. All the signs were there. I know those signs. Cat an' mouse innit. Don't need to verbal it. You just know wha' happens next. You know tha' right. It's like instinct. A fifth sense. You na'm sayin'. What can I say. You knew it. I knew it. Cat an' mouse. But which is which? Right?

Kissing noises. I try to block out the sound. The light in the bathroom trances my eyes with a million bottles an' jars of stuff all over hangin' in baskets or round the tub on shelves. Coloured creams an' gels an' oils for legs an' arms an' hair in the nose the ear an' the ass. Stuff for dry skin greasy skin hair straightener curl relaxer rinses dyes an' a loada shit for normal types whoever they are. Then there's brushes flannels stones razors. An' nail scissors.

I could change my hair to green stick a safety pin in my ear maybe even slice my wrists for that psychojerk effect. Then freak the fuck out of Baba. Only it wouldn't freak nobody cos it makes no difference. Only one thing does. I slip the scissors into my pocket.

Beyond the door the kuf musta kicked in cos Baba's a babblin' fool. An' Char's laughin' with him.

— So wha're these then? she says.

— Them's my love handles innit. I was always a bit porky. Even as a kid. But so what. The kids that got messed around at school cos they was wideload they was unhappy with themselves in the first place. Me I just took a look round my family. Na mean. They all weighed in at fifteen plus. Brothers sisters you name it. Only takes two of them to fill out the four seater in the livin' room. They're all *larger than life*. You know. Livin' it full throttle. One happy BIG family. Na mean. Me I've always been sixteen give or take a few pound. I'm truly stabilised now. Yeah trust me. Thing is I was even born *unnaturally big*. Thass what the doctor said *unnaturally big*. Accordin' to my gran. An' he must have been totally *rinsed* by *her* vitals. Coulda held the Queen's tea party under her skirt y'na mean. Her blouse was a parachute. Forklifts used to ferry food between her teeth. I loved her. Popped her clogs years back. Left a fair size hole in my life na mean. You don't forget someone like that. Someone who's dished out goodness an' nothin' but. Someone who's always there for you when it matters. She had a big heart y'na mean. Bigger the batty bigger the heart innit. My mum had half the batty an' she used to whoop us like we was war criminals. Which I guess we was. Even then...

More cluckin' an' kissin'.

— So you was all bad..., Char whispers.

— Yeah well, says Baba dredgin' up a smoky laugh, maybe we *were* a bit wild. An' just a bit porky...

I could puke down my front. I can't take no more. I'm still sweatin'. Only now it's fear pumpin'. A crowd of things shovin' round in my head. I'm standin' over the basin lookin' at elephant man in the mirror. Turn a tap an' throw some water on my face. Some perfume catches my eye so I spray it wherever there's a smell on me which is pretty much all over. I think about stashin' my paperwork in an old tin of talcum powder. But if I make it out I'll need it. My cigarettes must be on the kitchen table. Then I gargle with mouthwash til my eyes water. I hear Baba's muffled voice:

— Wha' the fuck was tha'?

— Wha' was wha'? says Char sleepy.

— Who you got in there? says Baba laughin'. Don't hold out...

— Just my mum an' my psychiatrist exchangin' notes. Na mean. Nothin' to worry about...

Baba laughs. Guess there's not much else to do short of takin' a bath. So I flush the toilet down hard an' walk out.

Char an' Baba're on the sofa all arms an' legs with pain an' horror on their faces like a spot-the-ball picture. Or like they just seen the Terminator rise out of green acid. They follow me with their eyes. I pass them headed for the kitchen an' front door. Baba's sayin' somethin' an' gettin' up. He's stark naked reachin' for Char's towel. The door's no more than a dozen steps. Char's shoutin'. Baba's paddin' up behind. I feel his breathin' on my neck before his hand lands on my shoulder. I sort of buckle but stay on my feet.

— Baba no, says Char.

But it ain't from the bottom of her soul. I turn an' look into his dead eyes. All round them there's tiny veins poppin' an' weird charlie twitches goin' on. He's figurin' not what to do but how. All I know's that standin' there all flabby an' bare like a bearded baby he hesitates. An' I wack him in the cheek with the point of the scissors. They go in deep an' sort of stick til the weight of my hand draws them out. His carcass kinda sways. I back off half waitin' for him to strike but he looks *bizarre*. Like he's just taken fifty thousand volts in the head. Like he's had too much happiness in his life. I let go the scissors wonderin' if I should finish him. I don't know what I should be doin'. I know what he'd do. Never turn down a free revenge.

Then Charmaine's in the way pushin' me back. Screamin' somethin'. Makin' no sense. I grab her throat with one hand to shut her up more than anythin'. Not that anyone'd listen up to another screamin' bitch on a fucked up estate. A hundred heads're buryin' in a second in a hundred pillows an' a hundred sleepy windows're pulled shut. Here I am watchin' her squirm confused at the end of my arm with the fear inside her. I raise my other hand. Then I'm walkin' cross the grass to Fola's car smokin' down a cigarette.

Nood'd be thinkin' now about how Baba'll do to Char what I couldn't. How a second later he'll be phonin' in back-up an' comin' after me. How Lendon'll sort Baba with the business end of his handgun. How one day someone'll arrange for Lendon to slip on a big banana skin. How all the phone numbers shoppin' an' paperwork'll need rearrangin'. An' how when all's said an' done there's got to be somethin' left for someone smart to collect. Someone like Nood. As for me it's time to sift an' be gone. If I could.

Fola swings the door open grinnin' then shocked.

— Where is tha jacket?

I get in. The car smells of armpits.

— Sold it to a fashion victim from planet pussy.

— What ah you saying?

— Had to ditch it. Sorry about that.

— You had to ditch my silvah killah–

I squeeze him another fifty.

— Deposit. I'll get it back for you. Jus' drive man...

I lean in close an' whisper.

— We're in danger...

Fola looks round left an' right in a panic pockets the fifty an' turns the ignition.

— You will get tha jacket? he says doin' a massive clutchburn start to let everyone know we're on our way.

— Yeh yeh...

— You will retrieve my propahty?

— Yeh yeh.

— You will keep yoh word?

— My word is my bond.

But he ain't *to-tahly* convinced shakin' his head an' cussin' to himself. He cruises distressed without a word all the way into Harlesden before he gets back to his groove.

— What do you say we go pahtee in tha Lov Box. It is jost ahround tha corner. Drown tha sorrows of this dark night. Ease lov tenshon. Monday babes ah jost tha best. No satahday night dollahgrabbahs. You know what I–

— Yeh less go celebrate good times.

With that Fola's awake again canin' it like he's got the winnin' ticket. He pulls out a fat skunk spliff for me to inspect.

— *To-tahly* yeah a'right danceyboy.

We come out into the one way reflectin' sleek in shop windows an' shoot past the clock tower with papers an' trash flyin'. The car's creatin' an evil wind that breaks the heat in two. I lean my head through the window an' open my mouth hopin' it's gonna blow the life out. But it don't.

Time flies

It's well late but the Lovebox kinda stays open for those who know. Ain't no flyers posters secret codes on walls about it. It ain't in no entertainment guide. Fact it ain't nowhere 'cept in the instinct of anyone anywhere gaggin' for a buzz. In the backstreet there's all kinds all over the pavement or sittin' on cars. Makin' calls. Billin' up. Soundin' off. Massives from the east. Funky dreds. Ponytails with rockchicks. A coupla Dorises. Ruff yoot. An' regular trippy smiley posse types. It's Kickback City where the only rule is to kick back.

We drift by an' park up. Fola gives his hair some wet look an' grabs some gold chains from under the rubber mat on the floor where he stashes it while workin'. I leave him to get his image together an' start toward the crowd.

From the Box there's bass spillin' an' a ball of heat at the entrance like it was microwave inside. People're emergin' out streetside sweaty an' fucked. I'm minglin' in with the crowd just siftin' up to the entrance when from a way behind I hear a VW van rumblin' up. Then metal screechin' on metal as its slide-door slides. I freeze knowin' the creakin' revvin' brakin' of this van better than my own face. This is the one place they're gonna look for me. But somehow I always knew that.

To the front a couple of bozo doormen stand with their hands clasped over their little dicks both of them suckin' on their teeth like yardies. They look me over as I step up.

— We got a policy, says Little Dick One.

— I'm on the list, I say brash.

— Fuck you is, says Little Dick Two. Whassamatter? Y'sister slap y'down?

They give their bodies a shake like they're laughin'. Then Fola arrives wide an' bright like a dancefloor.

— Folafreedom bring joy, he says pullin' the tips of his collar in the air then slappin' my back.

He shakes with both Dicks bungin' them ten apiece. They tick their heads toward the inside. Fola slips through into the UV light his white jeans glowin' all over. I stop a second about to look back.

— You in or wha'? says Dick One.

I nod an' step inside.

— They're on the list, he shouts to the droopy purple Gothchick behind the ticket table.

— Hands.

She takes our hands one at a time tryina protect what's left of her cracked blue nails an' stamps them with a faded red heart in a box. She points down the stairs into a cloud of dry ice. Ain't nothin' to do but go down.

— A'right man pahtee. Jost watch Folafreedom on the floor. Watch me spoonin' sugah. Smashing.

So we hit the stairs. A teenage kid with a stripey t-shirt to his knees passes us comin' up.

— Y'alrigh'? he says without lookin'.

— Wha' y'got?

— Wha' y'after? Special K. Es... Apples. Got some killer Doves.

Fola an' me take a look at the Doves smile at each other an' he takes out some dough.

— My pahtee ok.

I shrug.

— Can't argue with 'a', says the kid takin' a couple of tens. Nice one amigo. La'ers...

Past a plastic flap at the bottom of the stairs it's night of the livin' dead at two hundred beats a minute. The bass feels like it's gonna bust out my chest. The poundin' floor's vibratin' my eyeballs givin' me double vision. Special illuminoomi lights flash all over. Blue spot on a couple of raggastyle asses on a stage. The rest is wire bodies in shadows against fluorescent curvin' walls spraypainted with messages from beyond the grave:

FUCK THE PHAT AND RINSE OUT.

But rinsin' time is over. They're already in the crowd. I can feel them. Already siftin' behind us as we're movin' through. Deeper in another room lit red people're crashed left an' right smokin' an' rollin' with each other so's we're steppin' over them. They given top billin' to a fuckin' feedback hippy with an electric guitar singin' *peace an' love an' love yourself an' nobody else.*

Fola's puffed out scannin' for talent wavin' an' smilin' at strangers an' takin' licks from a half bottle of whisky. He's grabbin' spliffs tokin' 'em up an' passin' 'em back. Groovin'. Movin'. Superflyin'. Way out on his own.

An' so am I. On another day I could have been with him. Now I'm just gonna let him go. Like everyone else. Ain't nothin' I can do. Baba an' the psycho horde are closin' in. There's no silence. Never will be til it's over. But I don't give a fuck no more. I take the E hopin' it ain't aspirin. I'm livin' big. An' I come from Kilburn.